Eerey Tocsin in the Cryptoid Zoo

Written by
Kevin Noel Olson

Illustrations by
Debi Hammack

Eerey Tocsin in the Cryptoid Zoo
by Kevin Noel Olson

A Cornerstone Book
Published by Cornerstone Book Publishers
An Imprint of Michael Poll Publishing
Story Copyright © 2006 & 2015 by Kevin Noel Olson
Illustrations Copyright © 2006 & 2015 by Debi Hammack

Cornerstone Book Publishers
New Orleans, Louisiana

First Cornerstone Edition - 2006
Second Cornerstone Edition - 2015

www.cornerstonepublishers.com

ISBN:1613422423
ISBN-13:978-1-61342-242-7

MADE IN THE USA

Table of Contents

Dedication

This book is dedicated to my very own expert in caring for strange creatures.

— K.N.O.

Man looks in the abyss, there's nothing staring back at him. At that moment, man finds his character. And that is what keeps him out of the abyss.

— Hal Holbrook

Introduction

What I was doing at the Cryptoid Zoo seemed obvious, since that is where I traveled after I leant my plane to some friends. I hoped I could help them out. How I awoke in a cage I do not recall. Piecing events together from Eerey's diary, I now know why the air was thick with acrid smoke. At the time, I only knew that the caged animals would die from smoke inhalation if I didn't get them out of their cages. .

Returning to the Cryptoid Zoo for more research, I could at least verify much of Eerey's story by encountering various strange creatures mentioned in her diary, although I could not confirm the existence of the convenience store clerk. The profusion of male creatures over females in the events described might seem on its face quite confusing. While it may seem strange that aside from her mother, Eerey is the only representative of her gender, the explanation is very simple. Despite its simplicity, the explanation is also very, very long. Rather, we might take Eerey at her word when she purports, "Boys are dumb," and leave it at that.

If a genie granted me one wish it would be that you enjoy this story very, very much. If I were allowed another wish from the genie, I would wish you wouldn't blame me if you dislike the book. If I had a third wish granted, I would wish to be rich beyond my wildest dreams. In all seriousness, I probably would wish that first.

Sincerely,
Kevin Noel Olson

Illustrations

1.) **Eerey Tocsin**
Species: Purportedly human
Height: Still growing
Abilities: Sees well in the dark.

2.) **Edict Tocsin**
Species: Possibly hirsute human
Height: Still growing hair
Abilities: Jumps well in the dark.

3.) **Eightball** (spider size of a small dog)
Species: Megarchne
Size: Chihuahua
Abilities: Moves fast in the dark.

4.) **Loofah** (orangutaur)
Species: Orangutaur
Size: Small horse, large orangutan
Abilities: Smells bad in the dark.

5.) **Atlanta** (giant bird-big enough to carry a truck)
Species: Unknown big bird
Size: Extremely large for a big bird
Abilities: Carries heavy freight aloft in the dark.

6.) **Judge**-<Storsjöodjuret> (giant lake monster)
Species: Unidentified lake monster
Size: Average size for giant lake monster
Abilities: Swims well in the dark.

7.) **Mongolian Death Worm**
Species: Mortus Wormus
Size: Two meters long
Abilities: Electrocutes people in the dark.

8.) **Mothman**
Species: Neither a moth nor a man
Size: Man-sized
Abilities: Flies screaming in the dark.

9.) **Guy Guess** (invisible boy)
Species: Unforeseeably human
Height: Still growing, from what can be seen.
Abilities: Remains to be seen in the dark.

10.) **Asentizio** (leader of the Morlocks)
Species: Morlock
Size: Man-sized
Abilities: Leads Morlocks in the dark.

11.) **Giant chameleon crocodile**
Species: *Sarcosuchus imperator*
Size: Crocodiles are big, and this one's a giant one.
Abilities: Blends in with the color of its surroundings.

12.) **Giant Bats**
Species: Big Bakka (in Swedish)
Size: Huge-for bats.
Abilities: Screeches in the dark.

13.) Mister Cryptic
Species: Apparently human
Size: Tall
Abilities: Unclear in the dark.

14.) **Torrance, the Minotaur**
Species: Toro sapiens
Size: 8-boy's shoe
Abilities: Bull-headed in the dark.

15.) **Pen** (evil doppelganger-looks like Mr. Cryptic but with rows of sharp teeth)
Species: Doppelganger
Size: Mood-variable
Abilities: Changes in the dark.

16.) **Bigfoot**
Species: Sasquatch
Size: Shoes unavailable
Abilities: Tracks mud in the dark.

17.) **Morlocks**
Species: Morlocks
Size: Man-sized
Abilities: Sound scary in the dark.

18.) **Tyrannosaurus Rex** (Pen's transformation)
Species: Tyrannosaurus Rex
Size: King-sized dinosaur
Abilities: Eats well in the dark.

19.) **Eerey's Parents**
Species: Uncertainly human
Size: People-size
Abilities: Lose sight in the dark.

Eerey Tocsin in the Cryptoid Zoo

CHAPTER 1
A LETTER FOR MISTER CRYPTIC

Dear Mr. Cryptic,
My name is Eridona Tocsin, but my friends call
me Eerey. Because of my interest in hidden animals
like Bigfoot and Nessie, I purchased your book
*Cryptozoology: The Hunt For Strange and Unknown
Animals*. I enjoyed it very much.
I want to ask you a question about my cousin. Like
everyone born in the Tocsin family, he and I share
the same birthday. He is the strangest boy you will
ever meet. He has hair everywhere, and is the
weirdest little troglodyte that would ever grace a
cage at a zoo.
I sometimes wonder if he and I are really related.
He acts like the most uncouth creature. Since you
deal with unusual animals in your business, I hope
you might have some advice on how to handle
him.
Sincerely,
Eridona Tocsin

Eerey signed her name on the bottom of brittle yellow
stationery. As she folded the paper in the extremely dim light of
her room, the five-watt light bulb hanging from the ceiling
flickered slightly and went dark for a brief moment. Eerey always
had to explain to her parents why she kept her room so dark.
Darkness frightened her so she wanted to keep her eyes
accustomed to it. That made it easier to see what roamed about
at night.

Her parents always objected when the issue arose, so she
would often point her familiarity with darkness helped her find
her favorite pet. Her parents shuddered whenever Eerey brought

up the issue of the enormous spider living in her room, and they quickly changed the subject.

After pushing the lenses of her horn-rimmed glasses closer to her eyes, she brushed a long, dark-red curl of hair away from her olive-skinned features. With graceful fingers, she straightened the hem on her ankle-length white dress and pulled at its severe neckline.

Eerey insisted on wearing white dresses so other people could find her in the dark should the power fail. Other people did not see as well in dim light. She preferred used clothes and outdated fashions to newer styles. The many textbooks she'd read for school failed to show her how changes in fashion improved the world in any real way.

With a sigh, she meticulously re-read the letter. A corner flecked off as she held the fragile paper, but she paid no attention. She found the antique stationery in the basement of her house and decided it was still good. Anything was better than wasting useful items.

Satisfied with the message, she slipped the letter carefully into an old envelope. She addressed the envelope to Mr. Cryptic at the *Cryptoid Zoo*. In his book, Mr. Cryptic assured that all parcels addressed thusly and containing proper postage would reach him at the zoo.

Eerey lit a red candle and let the wax drip on the closed flap. She impressed the hot wax with a large 'T' from a ring on her left pinkie to represent the Tocsin family name. After some research, Eerey discovered Tocsin meant a warning sign or an omen, rather than something toxic and dangerous.

Taking the envelope in hand, she pushed away from the desk and glanced into the corner where Eightball rested. She'd named the spider Eightball because of its shiny, black surface and strange white marking on its underside. Eerey often pointed out to her parents that Eightball wasn't really all that large compared to a dog. In fact, their pet Chihuahua might someday become bigger than him. Eerey hadn't seen the Chihuahua around for a while, but she had never felt comfortable around it. Dogs were far too unpredictable.

Her parents would have killed Eightball when she first found him. The spider proved resistant to pesticides and had thick skin like a tick. This made him virtually indestructible. After a long and convincing argument made by Eerey on the spider's behalf, they agreed to allow her to keep him as a pet.

Her white dress reflected brightly as Eerey walked out of her room. She blinked at the yellow sunlight filling the hallway of her family's two-story, century-old home. She heard Eightball skittering in the darkness behind her. She shut the door to her room and started down the stairway.

As Eerey was halfway down the stairs, the antique banister shook violently. She rolled her eyes as Benedict slid down. He jumped off the railing at the bottom and waited for her.

Edict's hair-covered face beamed at Eerey. The golden, slightly curly hair hid everything but dark eyes, his long nose, and a wide grin. He wore a black suit and tie complete with a white shirt. He looked a little bit like a wolf in human clothing. More than that, he looked every bit like a werewolf from an old movie.

"Whatcha got there, cuz?" Edict asked, effortlessly keeping his broad grin alive as he spoke. Eerey hated it when he called her 'cuz'. It made her sound as if she represented a shortened version of the word 'because'. Even when her parents had brought him home on her seventh birthday and his sixth, some weeks after his parents mysteriously disappeared on the night of a full moon, he called her 'cuz'. He had said that nearly every day since.

"I am going to mail a letter," she replied sternly through pursed lips, "as if it's any of your business, Benedict."

Benedict did not notice her unpleasant tone. "Oh?" his smile grew impossibly wider. "It just so happens I'm going to the store. I'll take the letter to the post office."

"No, Edict," Eerey sighed. Her eyes softened as she shook her head. "I need to take this down myself, but thanks anyway."

"I'm going right by there," Edict reminded her. "It's not a

problem. The sun's out. I know how much it hurts your eyes."

She squinted as she saw the sunlight coming through the windows. Closing her eyelids, she rubbed them with the insides of her wrists. Without her sunglasses, the trip would be painful. It would be a couple of days before she could get her mother to take her to the junk shop to find another pair. She thought about Edict's offer for a moment.

"Okay, Edict," she consented. "I don't think my eyes can handle that much sunlight today. Just make sure the letter gets delivered, please."

Edict smiled kindly as Eerey walked the rest of the way down the stairs. She handed the letter out to Edict, but held on tightly when he grasped it. Edict looked at Eerey.

"Promise me it will get there," Eerey repeated.

"Certainly," Edict assured. "You have my word of honor!"

Eerey relinquished her hold on the letter. She gave Edict a half-smile. "Thank you," she said as she held forth a crumpled five-dollar bill. "You can keep the change."

He opened the front door and looked back at her. "You're welcome," he said with a wink. "I'll do anything for my favorite cousin! By the way, I'm really sorry about your sunglasses." Before Eerey could reply, Edict shut the door behind him. Eerey stared at the wooden door for a moment before returning to the oppressive darkness of her room.

Edict Tocsin

CHAPTER II
EDICT AND THE CRYPTOID ZOO

Edict walked down the street toward the post office with Eerey's envelope and five-dollars in hand. He whistled a haunting tune as he walked along. Many people on the street avoided Edict, but he remained cheerfully unaware.

He stopped in the convenience store to buy a candy-bar and a soda pop. As he stood at the register, he saw a comic book next to it. The latest issue of *Barricademan* was out. Edict grinned as he put the book in with the rest of his purchases.

It was not until he stood outside that he realized his mistake. He stopped and frowned. He had accidentally used Eerey's five-dollars. He'd spent all the money and couldn't send her envelope. He opened the bottle of pop and took a large gulp. How would he keep his word of honor, and deliver the letter safely?

As he thought about this, a large, white moving van with the words *Cryptoid Zoo* written on the side pulled up to the store's gas pump. The driver got out and began filling the tank. Edict's plan hatched in an instant.

When the driver went into the store to pay for the fuel, Edict casually walked to the back of the truck and pulled at the handle. The door opened. Edict moved back as a low growl escaped from one of the pair of cages the van held. Inside one of the cages, he saw a strange-looking creature with the torso and arms of an orangutan, connected to four legs and body of a horse. The other cage was empty except for a pile of straw.

Edict smiled after recovering from his initial shock. "A centaur," he commented to himself in a delighted tone. "Or at least, it's like a centaur. It must be an orangutaur," he mused, "but I've never heard of one of those."

Edict looked at the address on Eerey's letter. He walked to the side of the van to double-check. Satisfied the letters on the van and the address on the envelope matched, he climbed into the van and shut the door. A small light resting in the center of the van's ceiling provided a dull yellow glow.

He could hear the door of the van open as he climbed into the empty cage. The orangutaur growled lowly, but Edict took the candy-bar out of his pocket and removed the wrapper with the words *Chocolate Chasville Gnaw* written on it. He broke the candy bar and gave half to the creature. The orangutaur snatched the snack from Edict's hand and concentrated on the piece of chewy candy.

Edict did not know how far away the Cryptoid Zoo was, but it didn't worry him. He chewed on his piece of candy as he retrieved the comic book from his pocket and began to read. The battle between the comic's hero, Barricademan, and a villainous alien proved quite engaging for a while. He finished reading the book. He put it back in his pocket and drifted off to sleep on the straw.

He awoke when the back door to the van squeaked open. Sunlight flooded into the back of the van. Edict saw the heavyset driver from the convenience store, wearing the same dark-blue jumpsuit and matching baseball cap. Edict could see trees and a grassy lawn behind the driver. He pushed on the door of the cage, but found it had locked automatically when he'd shut it.

The driver's eyes widened when he saw Edict. "Where did you come from?" he said to Edict. He turned his head before Edict could answer and looked away from the van.

"Hey, Pendragon!" the driver shouted to the side of the van. "I thought I was just hauling an orangutaur! I've got a *Cro-Magnon* caveman or something here!"

"I'm not a *Cro-Magnon*!" Edict objected. He pulled violently at the lock.

"Hey, it talks!" the driver said. "What do you make of it, Pen?"

A thin man about seven feet tall walked over and stood next to the driver. Edict decided this must be the one called Pen. Pen's long, grey hair fell past his shoulders and crept like vines over his dark, grayish-purple suit. Together, the pair stared at Edict.

9

"He is right," Pen said finally. "He's not a *Cro-Magnon*."

"Thank you!" Edict sighed with relief. "I told you so."

"He's a *Combe-Cappelle* caveman," Pen decided. "He probably has ticks, too." Pen shuddered at the thought. "I hate arachnids!"

"No!" Edict shouted. "I'm not a *Combe-Cappelle* caveman either!" Eerey had taught Edict all about cavemen, so he knew something about the subject. "I'm human!"

"What are you doing in a cage then?" Pen sneered.

"I'm delivering a letter for my cousin," Edict replied. "As soon as I find Mister Cryptic, I'll be on my way."

"I'm Pendragon U. Cryptic," Pen offered. "That letter is for me."

Edict handed the letter to Pen through the bars of the cage. Pen opened the envelope and looked over the letter. Edict rested against the bars as he waited for Pen to finish.

Finally, Pen looked up at Edict with a nod. "Now I understand my mistake."

Edict crossed his arms. "That's good. You can let me out now that you know I'm human."

Pen shook his head. "My mistake was I didn't recognize your species. You're a troglodyte."

"A troglodyte's a type of ape," Edict protested. "I already told you; I'm not a caveman, and I'm not an ape! Besides, troglodytes and cavemen don't talk."

"I can familiarize you with any number of talking cavemen," Pen replied. "Cavemen and apes have many of the same potentials humans have."

Edict rolled his eyes. "I know some cavemen talk, but troglodytes still don't."

"Your own cousin says you're a troglodyte," Pen impressed. He held the letter to the bars for Edict to see. "See? It's irrefutable evidence."

This took Edict back as he read the letter. "I don't think she meant I'm really a troglodyte," Edict replied without conviction. It hurt his feelings that Eerey would say such things. Yes, he tormented her sometimes, but to be called a troglodyte? She could have at least called him a Neanderthal. "You won't want me to be a display at the zoo, will you?"

Pen smiled. "Of course we do! As you pointed out, troglodytes don't usually talk. I would be remiss in my duties as curator of this zoo if I didn't take the opportunity to include such a unique display."

"You can't keep me!" Edict snarled in protest. He shook the bars of the cage. "My family will come find me!"

Mr. Cryptic merely clapped his hands in delight. He looked at Edict with a particularly grim expression. "You failed to tell anyone where you were going, didn't you?"

Until that moment, Edict had a smug grin on his face. He quickly replaced this with a displeased frown. He realized Mr. Cryptic was right. Pen smiled broadly, displaying a row of sharp, white teeth.

"I'll tell the guests when they see me," Edict said.

"That's simple enough to remedy," Mr. Cryptic shrugged. "There aren't any guests at the Cryptoid Zoo. Even if there were, I could erase your memory. Then, you'd just be a talking troglodyte, and nobody else. It's not like the zoo will be around very long anyway."

"How can you erase my memory?" Edict asked.

"I have a doctorate in Mesmerism," Pen replied. "I can hypnotize anyone to think anything I want them to!"

Pen turned and walked away from Edict. Edict sat down on the straw and put his head in his hands.

Eightball

CHAPTER III

EEREY INVESTIGATES THE DISAPPEARANCE OF EDICT

After Edict left, Eerey read a book in the dimness of her room. Eightball curled up in her lap and slept like a cat, or a Chihuahua. She didn't think about the letter or Edict for about two hours, about the time she expected him to return.

"I wonder if Edict sent my letter yet," she said to Eightball. The spider merely growled a reply and rolled over in her lap. She returned to reading *Thirteen Terribly Deadly Mistakes and How to Avoid Ten of Them* and didn't think of Edict for another three hours or so.

It was long after sunset when Eerey remembered her cousin with a start. 'He should have been back by now,' she thought. 'I hope he mailed my letter.' She opened the door to her room and walked deftly down the darkened stairwell. She went to the kitchen where her mother was cooking dinner.

"Have you seen Edict?" Eerey asked.

Eerey's mother, startled by Eerey's voice, spun about quickly. "Oh Eridona!" she laughed. "You surprised me!"

"Have you seen Edict?" Eerey repeated. "I sent him to mail a letter this afternoon and expected him back by now."

"No," Eerey's mother replied. Her expression turned to one of concern. "How long has he been gone?"

"Since about two-thirty," Eerey replied. "It's dark outside, and he can't see in the dark as well as I can."

Eerey's mother nodded absently as she thought about what her daughter told her. "Perhaps we ought to go looking for him. I'll call your father. He's working late at the observatory."

"I'll see if I can find him," Eerey replied, though her mother failed to pay attention as she dialed the phone.

Eerey went to her room and got her backpack. She held it open next to Eightball, who slept curled up in a black clump. "Come on, Eightball," she said to the spider. "We're going to find Edict. Crawl in the bag."

Eightball's several eyes blinked wearily as he looked at the dark hole of the bag. His jaws spread wide as he yawned deeply. He let out a low growl before obediently climbing in. Eerey zipped the backpack and put it over her shoulders.

When she went downstairs, Eerey heard her mother on the phone. "Listen, this is Verna Tocsin," she said in a frustrated tone. "I need to speak to my husband Victor." Eerey walked out the front door and into the gloom of the moonlit night.

The dull glow from the streetlamps thrust through the bare branches of the trees. Eerey thought they provided too much light and wished she had her sunglasses. The lamps hid too many things in the darkness.

Eerey retraced what she suspected to be Edict's path. She headed toward the convenience store. Edict did say he planned to buy something on the way. He must have stopped there first.

When she arrived at the store, she walked up to the poorly-shaven clerk standing behind the counter. He wore a food-stained blue vest over a t-shirt. "Have you seen my cousin?" she asked.

The clerk looked confused. "Who?" he asked.

"My cousin Benedict," Eerey repeated. The clerk still looked puzzled, so she added, "He looks like a troglodyte."

"Oh!" the clerk said with a smile. "You mean the kid with all the hair?"

Eerey's heart jumped. "Yes! That's him! Did you see where he went?"

The clerk scratched his head. "Well," he began, "he came in and bought a comic book, a *Chasville Gnaw*, and a soda. The last time I saw him, he was outside looking at a moving van."

"What kind of moving van?" Eerey asked.

The clerk shrugged. "It had some writing on it."

"What did it say?"

His brow furrowed to indicate he was trying to recall. "I think it said something like '*Cryptoid Zoo*'."

Eerey now began to suspect what had happened. She asked

the clerk exactly what Edict purchased, and brought all the items to the counter. "How much does this all cost?"

"Say, that's exactly what the troglodyte bought!"

Eerey's eyes narrowed. "I know. How much do I owe?"

The clerk rang up her purchases. "Seven dollars even."

"Thank you." Eerey reached in her backpack, retrieved some neatly folded dollars, and handed them to the clerk. Edict had spent seven dollars on the items, but that didn't help Eerey much. Besides the five she'd given him she didn't know how much he had to begin with. Still, it might be useful information later. Eerey opened her backpack and pushed the growling spider gently aside.

"I've got to put these things in here," she said to Eightball. After she placed the items inside, the spider got comfortable again. She closed the backpack and slung it over her shoulder. She didn't know enough yet, but at least she'd found some clues.

She suspected Edict climbed into the van for some reason. Likely, he'd spent all the money and planned to deliver the letter by hand. He must have gone to the Cryptoid Zoo. Eerey thought she knew where Edict was. Unfortunately, she didn't know how to get there.

Loofah

CHAPTER IV
EDICT'S PREDICAMENT

Edict awoke in a cage, stretched across a bed of straw, without recollection of how he got there. Worse, he had no recollection of his own identity. The cage had two brick walls at the side and back and two rows of bars facing the path. The pile of straw on the floor completed the cage's contents, aside from a locked door in the back wall. He searched the entire cage with quick glances as he took stock of his new surroundings. The day was warm, but a welcome breeze of cool air blew the straw around in Edict's new quarters. "Wow!" he exclaimed aloud. "An adventure! This is awesome."

Deciding the cage quite trapped him, Edict went to the front bars. He looked down a narrow pathway lined with reddish-brick at other cages separated by considerable distance. Edict looked around for a person, but the pathway remained clear. Animals rested in the cages on the path, but Edict could not see them clearly from so far away. Dreary clouds strained the sunlight until only a dull grey light covered the ground.

The only cage with contents stood directly next to Edict's. The creature inside had the body and legs of a horse with the torso, head, and arms of an orangutan. Long, orange fur covered its body. For some reason the word 'orangutaur' came to Edict. He understood the word meant something like a cross between an orangutan and a centaur. Aside from that, it held no significance for Edict.

Finally, Edict grabbed the bars and yelled down the pathway. "Hey!" he shouted. "Can anybody hear me?"

The orangutaur stirred and rolled over on its bed of hay, but no other response came. Edict decided to repeat his shouting. "Hello!" he yelled. "I don't belong here! Why am I here?"

"Be quiet!" a voice said.

Edict looked around until his eyes rested on the orangutaur's cage. The orangutaur stood on its feet, glowering at Edict with his orangutan eyes. "What?" Edict said in surprise.

"I said keep it down!" the orangutaur repeated. "Most of us are trying to sleep!"

Edict stared at the orangutaur. "I didn't know you could talk."

"You never asked if I could talk."

"We've never met before," Edict objected. "I don't know how I could have asked."

The creature's eyes narrowed and it curled its lips threateningly. "We've never met? We met yesterday in the moving van! You can't deny it."

Edict shook his head in confusion. "I'm not denying it, but I don't remember it."

The orangutaur peered at Edict suspiciously. "You really don't remember meeting me?"

"Honestly," Edict replied, "I don't remember anything but waking up in this cage."

"Well then," the orangutaur said, "you may need my help. My name's Loofah."

"You would help me?" Edict asked.

"You gave me a gift yesterday," Loofah replied. "I'm actually indebted to you."

"What did I give you?"

"A candy bar, but that's not the point. An orangutaur has honor, and I didn't have to accept your gift. Since I did, I 'owe you one' as humans like to say."

"Can you tell me who I am and how I got here?"

Loofah shrugged his powerful shoulders. "You didn't say who you were, and I didn't ask. As far as how we got here, we came in a moving van. They probably flew the van here in an airplane, because the Cryptoid Zoo is on an island. As for not talking before, I didn't want you to know I could speak."

"You're letting me know now," Edict pointed out.

"Well, we're both in the same boat now, aren't we?"

Edict nodded his agreement.

"Being an orangutaur's bad enough without talking too.

Everyone wants to capture you. Let's not get into that," the orangutaur continued, "I can tell you some things you said yesterday. You told Mister Cryptic..."

"Mister Cryptic?"

"Yes," Loofah sighed. "He's the curator of the zoo. You met him earlier, and you'll meet him later. You told Mister Cryptic yesterday that your cousin sent you. You said she wanted you to deliver a letter."

"What's her name?" Edict asked.

"Whose name?"

"My cousin's."

Loofah shook his head. "I don't know. You never said that, either."

"What did I say?"

"You said you weren't a caveman, or a troglodyte. Mister Cryptic showed you your cousin's letter, which apparently said you were a troglodyte. Unfortunately, I didn't get to read it."

Edict rubbed his chin, trying to solve the riddle beginning to form in front of him. "Where did the letter go?"

"I don't know. Mister Cryptic kept it, I suppose. Then, he threatened to erase your memory."

"So he's hypnotized me to forget," Edict mused. Then he turned to Loofah. "Am I a troglodyte?"

Loofah shrugged. "Maybe. You look a bit like one. Troglodyte's aren't supposed to talk, though."

"Are orangutaurs?"

"I don't know," Loofah admitted. "I'm the only orangutaur I've ever met."

"We've got to get out of here," Edict decided. "Do you have any ideas?"

"Not really," the orangutaur admitted, "but I'm trying to think one up. I know it'll be a great one when I do. Maybe..." He seemed prepared to continue, but suddenly fell quite silent. Edict saw a man in a blue jumpsuit walking down the pathway. He pushed a cart full of vegetables.

Loofah rushed to the bars of the cage, thrusting his arms as far as they would go past the bars. He seemed quite eager as the man approached him with a banana. Loofah made puffing orangutan noises of approval as he snatched the banana from the attendant's hand. He retreated to the corner of the cage and acted very much more like an orangutan than he had previously. Edict figured Loofah was literally playing dumb for the zookeeper.

The zookeeper approached Edict with a handful of carrots. "Here you go, boy. Eat up." He held out the carrots to Edict. His name was Jack according to the tag on his shirt. Jack had driven the van that brought Edict and Loofah to the zoo, but Edict didn't remember that.

Edict hit the carrots, knocking them onto the pathway's red bricks. "I don't want carrots!" he yelled. He pressed his face threateningly against the metal bars. Loofah gave him a warning glance, but Edict did not see it. "I want out of here! I can talk, and I can think!"

Jack looked surprised for a moment. Then, the zookeeper laughed. "We have plenty of talking animals," he said. Jack's surprise was at Edict's refusal of the carrots and not at his ability to speak. "You're not going anywhere." Jack reached into the cart and pulled out some potatoes.

"I don't want anything," Edict said with a frown.

Jack put the potatoes back in the cart. "You will when you get hungry," he replied. He continued to push the cart down the pathway.

After Jack disappeared behind a turn in the path, Loofah turned to Edict. "You're not going to get anywhere by refusing food," he admonished. "You should eat everything they give you. You'll need your strength if we're going to escape."

"Do you have a plan?" Edict asked.

"Of course I have a plan!" Loofah said emphatically. "I'm an orangutaur!"

"Okay, okay," Edict said. "I apologize. It's just that you said you didn't have a one earlier. Tell me your plan." Loofah and Edict started to plan their escape together.

Atlanta

CHAPTER V
EEREY SENDS A PACKAGE

Eerey went home and fell asleep. Without telling her parents, she'd formulated a plan to retrieve Benedict. Telling them would simply cause needless worry.

In the morning, Eerey brushed her teeth and hair then put on a white dress. She went to her room and packed her backpack. She included Mr. Cryptic's book, a large amount of money she had been saving, some *Chasville Gnaw* candy bars, her mother's cell phone, and Eightball. The spider grumbled incoherently at the cramped area when Eerey placed him inside the backpack. Eerey attributed this irritation on Eightball's part to the untimely hour of the morning.

Eerey's parents were gone by the time she prepared to leave. Doubtless, they were searching for Edict. After a breakfast of tea and toast, she wrote a short note for her parents. She attached the note to the refrigerator and left the house.

Eerey put on sunglasses she borrowed from her mother as the bright light began to make her eyes hurt. She took the same path she supposed Edict took the day before. She continued past the convenience store without stopping. She did not stop until she arrived at the post office.

At the post office, she purchased a large, wooden crate and proper postage from the clerk. She retrieved Mr. Cryptic's book from her backpack. Eightball growled in protest, but quickly returned to sleeping. Eerey opened the book and wrote the address of the Cryptoid Zoo on the outside of the box with a black marker. She wrote a short letter and included it in the empty crate. The contents of the letter were as follows:

> Dear Mr. Cryptic,
> It is my belief that somehow my cousin Edict has ended up at your Zoo. I have included proper

postage for his return trip in this crate. Please package him correctly and return him as soon as possible. He and I have a birthday celebration in the near future, and his absence would not do.
Sincerely,
Eridona Tocsin
P.S. The candy bars are for Edict's return trip.

The clerk left for his break while she wrote the note. Eerey pushed the crate next to a drawer labeled *outgoing mail*. She bent into the crate to place the candy bars inside. As she did this, the lid of the crate fell and hit her on the back of the head, knocking her out. Unconscious, she slid into the crate with the lid closing behind her.

The postal clerk returned from lunch and saw the crate. With the postage already on it, he decided the package must be ready to go. He nailed the lid shut and slid it into the mailroom.

Eerey awoke to a low and quiet droning noise that filled the crate. She rubbed the knot on her head from where the lid hit her. The crate shifted slightly as if it something pushed at it. She pressed against the top of the crate, but it remained shut despite her best efforts. She could not see either. The crate didn't allow any light to enter.

Taking off her backpack, she unzipped it and let Eightball out. The noise and abject darkness frightened the large spider. It curled up on Eerey's shoulder for comfort. Eightball quickly fell asleep again and snored loudly.

Eerey turned her attention to re-examining the crate. She felt around the inside, pressing the wood with her hands. Splinters poked at her fingertips as she ran them along the inside. Finally, she found an indentation in the side of the box. It felt like someone had placed a sticky piece of paper over the hole. She tore a hole in what must be some kind of label.

Dim yellow light poured through the newly created opening. It appeared to be a handhold to assist in carrying the crate, and Eerey checked the other side to confirm an identical hole covered with a sticky label.

Eerey peered through the first hole into a long tube of a room. She recognized it from pictures as being the inside of a cargo plane. Eerey had become airmail.

The plane's engine noise was deafening. Eerey saw a pair of legs clad in black work jeans and shouted. The man wearing the pants couldn't hear her over the loud drone. Eerey felt the pressure change in the crate. She went to the other hole to see why. Pushing the label off she could see an enormous door opening to create a ramp at the back of the plane. She could see stars and moonlit clouds as she realized what was happening.

She heard the crate scrape along the bottom of the airplane as the man pushed it toward the hole. Suddenly, gravity took over the task. The crate began to roll on metal wheels in the floor toward the open night sky. Eerey's eyes widened as the crate approached the edge of an enormous drop.

Eerey quite needlessly stifled a scream as the wooden box fell into the open air. Though she had excellent vision for seeing in the dark nothing but moonlit clouds and stars remained visible as she felt the box begin to fall. Dropping below the clouds, it picked up speed very quickly. It reminded her of a very fast roller coaster she'd taken with her parents, but far more frightening.

She could see a fairy ring of small, twinkling of lights inside an ocean of darkness below. The moon illuminated the clouds above with a dull wash of dimness. Eerey watched as she rode the crate toward the small smattering of lights.

Suddenly, a loud whooshing sound came from above the crate. Something yanked at the wooden box, and it slowed to a more moderate and controlled pace. Eerey thought the whooshing sound came from an opening parachute at first, but it repeated itself at regular intervals. She didn't think the crate fell as if a parachute carried it, either. In fact, it felt as if the crate glided above the ground in a slow, circling descent.

She listened carefully to the whooshing noises. They made the sound of an enormous bird flapping its wings. She tried to look out the hole, but she couldn't see what was carrying the crate.

As the crate approached the ground, Eerey saw a circle of streetlights lighting a round patch of concrete. The crate continued to descend toward the lights. Finally, the crate landed on the pad of concrete. Though the landing was gentle, it still woke Eightball. The disoriented spider curled tightly around Eerey's upper arm.

"Nice landing, Atlanta," A man's voice said from outside the crate. Eerey saw a gargantuan bird land next to the crate on the concrete platform. Its wingspan might have been half a football field long by her estimation. She could not believe it, but this giant bird must have carried her crate to the ground. She remembered reading about giant bird sightings in Alaska, and wondered if she might be there.

Someone started to work at the top of the crate with a crowbar. The person stood on the side without the holes, so Eerey could not see them. She put Eightball in her backpack and waited. As soon as the lid came off, Eerey stood up.

A tall man dressed in a dark grayish-purple suit stepped back at Eerey's quick and unexpected motion. He leaned on a cane in his right hand. "Hello there," the man said as he smiled a display of sharp teeth. "I suppose we might have a Jacqueline in a box?"

"No," Eerey replied. "My name's Eridona." She took a deep breath and wiped dust from her dress.

The man's smile lessened. "Eridona Tocsin?" he asked. His smile returned as he offered his hand to Eridona. "Of course, of course! We've been expecting you!" Eerey did not take his hand, but offered an enigmatic smile.

"I am Pendragon U. Cryptic," the man continued. "I am curator of this menagerie of madness, but you may call me Pen. It's a pleasure to meet you."

"You can call me Eerey," Eerey climbed out of the crate without Mr. Cryptic's aid. "I am here to retrieve my cousin."

"Perhaps he does not want to be retrieved," Mr. Cryptic

replied. "You treated him unkindly in your letter."

"Perhaps I shall see for myself," Eerey said defiantly.

"Oh, you shall see for yourself, but only if I allow it."

"Will you allow it?" Eerey asked. It quite displeased her to feel dislike toward Mr. Cryptic, since she had felt a great respect for him before this meeting.

Pen rubbed his chin in consideration. "Perhaps I will," he said finally, "if you are willing to earn the privilege."

"How do I do that?" Eerey asked.

"By completing a series of tests," Pen replied. "They are of my design, and test your worthiness."

"I don't have to prove anything to you," Eerey challenged. "I am worthy to see my own cousin!"

Pen feigned a look of shock. He dramatically placed his fingers on his chest. "Oh my! It is not me you have to prove it to, Eerey." His eyes turned toward the ground as if he were about to say something difficult. "You see, it is your cousin. You made it plain you did not want him as your cherished relative any longer."

"I never said that," Eerey said quietly.

"Perhaps not," Pen agreed, "You certainly implied it."

Eerey took her backpack off. She rummaged through it without taking her eyes off Pen. "I'll call my parents," she threatened as she retrieved her mother's cell phone.

"Be my guest," Pen said with a smile.

Eerey dialed the number to her home. She was pleased that the call went through. Her mother answered, "Hello?"

"Hello mother," Eerey said.

"Eridona!" her mother said excitedly. "Are you all right? Where are you? Did you find Benedict?"

Eerey nodded, even though her mother could not see her. "I'm okay. I've found Benedict, and he's doing well too." Eerey glanced at Mr. Cryptic. He nodded his agreement. "We're at the Cryptoid Zoo."

"Where is that?" her mother asked.

"Just a minute." Eerey turned to Pen and asked, "Where

exactly is the Cryptoid Zoo?"

"Do you know where Albuquerque is?" Pen asked.

Eerey nodded. "It's in New Mexico."

"How about Wawa?"

"I don't know where that is."

"It's in Ontario," Pen replied. "Do you know where Walla Walla is?"

"I think it's in Washington. But none of them are anywhere near each other!"

Pen smiled. "That's exactly where the Cryptoid Zoo is. Not anywhere near any of them!"

"That's no help," Eerey protested.

"Help to do what, exactly?"

"Help my parents find us," Eerey said.

"Oh, I do not think there is any amount of help for that," Mr. Cryptic said. "If you cannot find yourselves, you ought not to place that burden on others."

Eerey frowned. Pen obviously refused to help her. She spoke to the phone once more. "Mother, don't worry about us. I'll get Benedict and bring him home. We'll be fine, I promise."

"Where are you?" her mother repeated.

Eridona simply replied, "We'll be fine, Mother. Please trust me."

The cell phone cut out as the battery died. Eerey put it back in her backpack. She looked at Pen. "Let's get on with the tests."

Judge - <Storsjöodjuret>

CHAPTER VI
THE TRIALS AND TRAVAILS OF EEREY TOCSIN

Pen led Eerey down a brick path lined with streetlamps. These threw a sallow light across the path. Eerey could see past the streetlamps enough to recognize limbs of trees to her right. The bare branches stretched toward the cloud-covered sky and the moon beyond. A large field of grass lined the side to her left, leading to a small lake.

"Where are we going?" Eerey asked Pen.

"Where?" he repeated. "Why, to your first test."

"How many tests will I have to take?"

Mr. Cryptic shrugged. "None," he said, "if you don't want to see your cousin, that is. On the other hand, if you do want to see your cousin…"

"I do," Eerey affirmed.

"Then you'll have to take as many as it takes, won't you?"

"How many will that be?"

"Three," Pen stated with frankness.

Eerey saw their destination before Pen pointed it out. "There," he said. "See the large indentation?"

Eerey nodded as they continued walking. A large, bowl-shaped pit with a wooden floor rested in the earth. A pair of wooden bumpers started at the edge about three feet apart and ran parallel down to a black hole in the bottom. A pair of gutters ran right next to the bumpers. Even in the dark, Eerey recognized the construction.

"It looks like a bowling alley," Eerey said, "twisted into a spiral." She saw twelve bowling pins placed singly at regular intervals all the way down the circular lane. Their placement varied from the center to either side.

Pen nodded. "It is a specially-built bowling alley based on ancient fossil snail shells."

"You mean ammonites, the spiraled fossil remains of shellfish."

"Exactly. This design came from a living ammonite we have in our aquarium. It has been supposedly extinct for years, like many of the animals we have here at the Cryptoid Zoo."

"Okay," Eerey said with an impatient tone. "I have to bowl in a lane built like a corkscrew."

"Yes. You have to knock down all the pins to pass this test."

"That's not possible," Eerey said.

"Those are the rules." Pen indicated a rack of bowling balls with the tip of his cane. "You can pick any you like."

"None of those will do, thank you," Eerey said with all possible politeness.

"Oh?" Pen's face grew curious. "How will you bowl, then?"

"I've brought my own bowling ball," Eerey assured. She took off her backpack and rummaged through it.

"Indeed," Pen said with a smile. "You have come prepared!"

Eerey turned her back a bit to Pen as she grabbed onto Eightball. Eightball grumbled, but she gave the spider a wink. "Play dead," she whispered. "We're going bowling." Eightball curled its legs around his body and shut his eyes.

"What is that you said?" Pen asked as he came closer to look at her bowling ball.

Eerey obscured the side with Eightball's legs by holding him against her dress. Only his smooth side showed. "Nothing," Eerey remarked. "Just a child's rhyme I recite." Pen looked at her sideways, so she added, "I'm a little superstitious, you know."

"May I examine that bowling ball?"

Eerey calmly shook her head. "No. Superstition, you know."

Pen sighed. "Very well. Go on and take your shot."

Eerey moved to the lane and Pen followed her. "Do you mind?" she said to him. "It's unlucky to have someone stand next to you."

Pen moved back until she stopped glaring at him. "Okay, Eightball. You know what to do." She grabbed onto Eightball, and he wrapped his legs around her fingers. The darkness provided little light, and Eerey hoped Pen could not see. She rolled Eightball down the lane as the spider released her hand.

The spider saw the first pin coming up on the left and stretched his legs into the gutter on that side. His legs could not miss the pin; he knocked it over with ease.

"Did you see that?" Pen asked.

"What?" Eerey asked. "Do you mean that shadow?" Even with her keen night-vision, she could not make out the spider's legs at this distance. Hopefully, Pen would not be able to either.

"Oh," Pen said. "Never mind."

Eerey stifled the urge to breathe a sigh of relief. She watched as Eightball managed to knock over white pin after white pin, all the while looking like an ordinary bowling ball in the darkness.

Eightball met the pins in the center head-on and knocked them over easily. It did not hurt his thick hide at all. He continued thrusting his legs out when pins were on the side. He soon came to the hole in the bottom of the large bowl and fell into it.

"You did it," Pen congratulated. "I have never seen anyone get all the pins before!" He smiled broadly, and Eerey could not tell if it delighted or angered Pen that she'd gotten all the pins.

"I won my junior bowling league championship," Eerey replied as she walked over and stood next to the bowling ball return.

"Junior bowling must have improved since I was a child," Pen admitted.

"I guess it must have." Eightball rolled out onto the conveyor belt. Eerey snatched the spider up quickly and put him in her backpack. Pen was not paying attention at any rate. He continued to look at the lane in amazement.

"So," Eerey broke into Pen's thoughts, "what's the next test?"

Pen turned. "Very well," he said, "although I may have to come up with something difficult now. Follow me."

Mr. Cryptic lead Eerey along the brick path. The path wound around until Eerey and Pen walked along the lakeshore. The clouds parted, allowing moonlight to filter through in long, white streams of luminescence. Light twinkled off the tiny waves in the lake.

"It's quite a nice lake," Eerey observed.

"Yes," Pen agreed. "We have to walk across it now."

"Walk across it?"

"We will not have to walk on water to do so." Pen pointed to individual rocks jutting from the water in a line across the lake. "However, we might have to make small jumps."

"Isn't there another way?"

"Not if you are to complete your next test." Pen stepped onto the nearest rock in the lake and then continued to the next. "Come on!" he exclaimed with childish glee. "It is a lot of fun."

While Pen fairly ran down the pathway over the lake, Eerey remained cautious. The distance between the rocks caused her to have to leap in many places, since her legs were not long like Pen's.

Eerey began to feel more confident at about the center point of the lake when she saw something moving beneath the dark water. She might not have seen it coming at all if not for her ability to see in the dark. She made out a giant serpentine form swimming beneath the water unlike any she had seen in real life. She began to run across the lake after Pen, heedless of the rocks.

"Pen!" she yelled. "It's the Loch Ness Monster!"

Pen, now nearly on the other shore, simply shook his head. He brought his hands face and cupped them around his mouth to yell a reply. "It's not Nessie!" he shouted.

Just then, an enormous green head atop a long neck thrust out of the water next to Eerey. It closely resembled the head of a green, hairless cat with a long, dinosaur neck. The head equaled a car in size, and perhaps weight. At least, Eerey hoped the creature was an herbivore, and did not eat meat like a carnivore or omnivore.

Eerey stifled a scream. She remained very still, but the time for stillness had passed. The lake monster had seen her. Its large black eyes blinked in the darkness as the moon reflected in their shiny surfaces. It looked directly at Eerey. Despite her greatest hopes it plunged its head toward her.

Eerey screamed as it opened its mouth and caught her in its teeth. The creature held her in its mouth, its teeth around her waist. She punched at its round nose, but it did not seem affected.

"Pen!" Eerey shouted as she looked in Mr. Cryptic's direction.

Eerey saw that Pen had already run part of the way back along the rocks towards the creature. "Hold on, Eerey!" he shouted. "I'm coming!" Eerey noted he didn't seem to be moving very quickly.

Eerey didn't feel as if she had all that much time to wait. The creature blinked its enormous eyes at her. At least the creature wasn't chewing on her yet. The thought gave her an idea. She reached into her bag and recovered a *Chocolate Chasville Gnaw*. She tore the wrapper off the candy bar and threw it into the creature's mouth.

It landed on its thick tongue. The tongue began to swirl the object around. As soon as the creature's taste buds started enjoying the flavor, it released Eerey and chewed on the tiny chocolate morsel.

Eerey took a deep breath as she fell into the water. She narrowly missed hitting the rocks as she plunged into the deep, dark lake. She recovered and began swimming toward the surface.

She found she had plunged a great distance into the water. The strenuous swim took energy out of her as she followed the moon's pale disc. She feared she might pass out before reaching the surface. As she neared the surface, she felt something grabbed her under the left armpit.

Pen used the crook of his cane to pull her out of the water. Eerey gasped for breath as he set her on one of the stepping-stones. She released a choking cough from the water and looked at the lake creature. It happily chewed on its *Chasville Gnaw*. 'It's a good thing the candy bars last a long time,' Eerey thought to herself.

When she had recovered, she looked at Pen. "Nessie nearly ate me!" she protested.

"I told you before; that's not Nessie," Pen replied. "He was not trying to eat you, either. He was merely being playful."

"Playful! He nearly bit me in two!" Eerey looked cautiously in her backpack to see if Eightball was okay. Waterproofing had kept the inside from getting wet and the spider slept soundly.

"Do you really suppose if an animal of that size with teeth that large tried to bite you in two it could not?" Pen asked, shaking his head. "No, if he wanted to eat you, we would not be having this conversation."

Eerey shuddered as she nodded. Pen's words made her less frightened of the creature and she thought now it was somewhat cute in an incredibly dangerous way. "If he's not Nessie, who is he?" she asked as Pen put his coat on her shoulders.

"He is a lake creature like Nessie, but not from Loch Ness. He is from a lake in Sweden. His mother's name is Storsjöodjuret."

"Store-judge-rat?" Eerey repeated.

"Close enough," Pen replied. "We named him Judge. We should get going before he wants to play some more."

Eerey stood and followed Pen across the lake. She shivered from the cold. "So, did I pass?" she asked between chatters from her teeth.

"Pass what?" Pen asked as he stepped from one rock to the next.

"The second test," Eerey said.

"Oh no," Pen replied. "That was not the second test."

Eerey frowned at this revelation, but said nothing as she followed Pen to the other side of the lake. Pen stepped off the last rock and walked along the brick path on the other side.

A steep wall of obsidian about twenty feet tall lined the path on this side. The sides of the rock were smooth as glass and black as pitch. The formations made an effective fence. Eerey took note of this. "Are those rocks obsidian?"

Pen nodded. "This area is volcanic. The walls of obsidian glass are an unusual but natural formation. It is virtually unheard of, in fact. The walls surround the entire zoo," Pen said proudly. "It's tall enough to keep the animals inside in, and to keep the animals outside out."

Eerey thought that might account for the fact she had never heard of such a thing. The obsidian wall went off in a different direction after some distance, and Eerey could see a field of short, green grass. It appeared to be a golf course by the appearance of tiny flags sprouting from the ground at various distances and directions. Mr. Cryptic stopped at the edge of an enormous sand trap a slight way into the green.

"This is your second test," Pen informed as he pulled the top off his cane to reveal a thin golf club. At the same time, his other hand produced a white golf-ball. "Take this putter, and hit the ball to the other side of the sand trap. You have to go over, or if you can't make it in one hit, through the sand trap."

Although it would be difficult to hit the ball all the way across with a putter, this test seemed too easy. Even if it took time, Eerey could continue hitting the ball until it left the sand trap.

"There is one other thing to mention," Pen broke into Eerey's thoughts. "The sand trap is infested with Mongolian death worms."

"What!" Eerey said. "Mongolian death worms? They spray poison, or release an electrical charge like an eel. They are deadly! You actually put them on your golf course?"

Pen shrugged. "It's the sand trap; it's not supposed to be easy. Besides, Mongolian death worms usually live in the Gobi desert, so our sand trap seemed an appropriate place to put them. It wouldn't be a challenge if all you had to do was watch out for the quicksand," he offered.

"Quicksand?" Eerey replied.

"Come now. Certainly, you would risk a little danger to have your cousin back?"

Eerey shrugged. She bit into her lip as she roughly grabbed the putter and golf ball from Pen. "You are not at all what I thought you would be," she grumbled. She set the golf ball on the ground and got into a stance to strike it.

Eerey swung at the ball. The putter hit the ball hard, but the white orb flew through the air and landed in the middle of the sand trap. Eerey looked at Pen and huffed. She turned back to the sand trap and began to walk cautiously toward the ball.

Eerey's vision allowed her to see in the darkness, but she did not know if a Mongolian death worm might burrow under the sand. In that case, she might not see one until it was close enough to spit its poison at her.

Eerey reached the golf ball without incident. She drew the putter back to take another swing. Suddenly, a large, red worm burst from the sand ten feet in front of Eerey. Eerey froze, looking at the four-foot worm closely resembling a large, bloated nightcrawler. It slithered quickly toward Eerey as she retreated backwards. After a few feet, the worm stopped moving. Eerey paused as well.

"Come here," the worm hissed in a quiet, scratchy sound. Eerey could not see the worm's mouth speak, but its body wriggled on the sand. The vibration it made against the sand seemed to form words. It sounded strange.

Eerey shook her head. "Worms can't talk."

"I can," the worm replied by shifting its body against the sand. "Mongolian death worms are different. Come here."

"What's going on out there?" Pen shouted.

"It's just a death worm," Eerey yelled back. She turned her attention to the worm. "You just want me to come closer so you can spit on me."

The death worm leaned back as if ready to strike, then spit out a stream of green liquid that went about five feet beyond and three feet over from where Eerey stood. It glowed against the yellow sand where it fell.

"I could easily hit you with poison now," the worm informed. "I just might, if you don't come over here."

Eerey gulped and walked toward the death worm. She came within a few feet of it before she noticed how bad it smelled. She had to hold her nose as the death worm whispered to her by wriggling against the sand. "That's not Mister Cryptic you're with," it said.

"What?" Eerey managed.

The death worm shook its head. "That's not Mister Cryptic, or at least not the Mister Cryptic who runs this zoo. That's a doppelganger."

Eerey forgot about the smell as she listened in amazement. "You mean like the shape-shifting doppelgangers that can look like anyone or anything? How do you know?"

"We worms have ears," the worm replied. "We hear everything that's said above ground. Pen kidnapped Mister Cryptic. He might capture you as he has your cousin. On the other hand, he may even kill you if you don't seem useful to him. He would not have sent you out here for us to kill if he needed you."

Eerey took the book out of her backpack and looked at the back cover. The words beneath the black-and-white photo read *Mr. Cryptic*. It displayed a man who looked exactly like Pen, except for the row of nice, straight teeth. Pen's teeth were pointed, sharpish and even sharkish.

"What do I do?" Eerey asked the worm, convinced that Pen was not the real Mr. Cryptic.

"I suggest you pretend to be dead," the worm replied. "Pen will think I've killed you with my invisible death-force."

Eerey did not know why she should trust a death worm, but she felt certain she could no longer trust Pen. As she considered, the Mongolian death worm let out its invisible death-force and delivered an electrical shock. It felt much like the time she stuck her finger on a wire with a short in it. The feeling ceased, and Eerey fell unconscious to the ground.

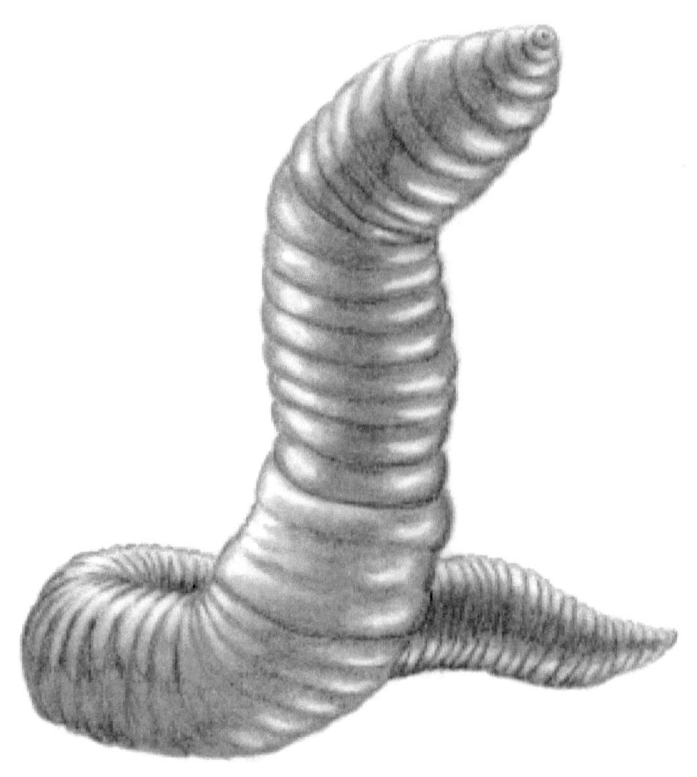

Mongolian Death Worm

CHAPTER VII
THE PLAN OF EDICT AND LOOFAH

"I don't think this has a very good chance of working, Loofah," Edict said to the orangutaur. The lamps illuminated the night as Loofah worked his cage, weaving a rope from his own hair. "It's a useless rope."

Loofah waved his hand dismissively. "Of course it'll work!" he insisted. He returned to weaving the pile of orangutaur-hair. "An orangutaur's plan always works!"

"Really?" Edict asked. "I'd never heard that before."

"How many orangutaurs have you met before?"

"None," Edict admitted. "How many plans have you had work before?"

"None," Loofah acknowledged, "but I've never made a plan before."

"How do you know if it will work if you've never succeeded?"

Loofah eyes narrowed. "Because," he growled, "I've never had a plan fail!"

"That could be because you've never had a plan to fail with."

"I don't see you offering to give up some of your hair," Loofah replied. "You've got plenty to give."

"Hey," Edict protested. "You don't have to get personal."

Loofah chewed on his lip for a moment. "I suppose you're right," he sighed finally. "There's no reason for us to fight. Let's just give this a try though, okay?"

Edict nodded. "Okay, but if it doesn't work, we ought to go with my plan."

"Neither of those plans will work," a voice interrupted from nowhere. Loofah and Edict looked about, but could not find the origin of the voice.

"Who said that?" Edict demanded.

"I did," the voice of unseen origin replied.

"Who are you?" Loofah said. "Better yet, where are you? Come into the light. We want to see you!"

"I'm standing under the lamp now," the voice offered. A low, buzzing noise like that of a bee accompanied the voice.

"No, you're not," Edict snarled. "We want to see you."

"You can't see me," the voice said, "because I am invisible. You can hear me, though. Isn't that enough?"

"I guess it will have to be," Loofah snorted. "What's that buzzing noise?"

"I am invisible," the voice returned, "but I'm not inaudible. Whenever I stand in the light I start to buzz."

"Why?" Edict asked.

"It's a type of interference," the voice replied. "Sort of like with a bad cell phone signal. My body has to work harder to appear invisible in the light, so it ends up transmitting a buzzing tone. I go off like a fire alarm in broad daylight."

"Can you prove that you're under the light?" Edict asked.

"Sure," the voice replied. The buzzing sound lessened for a moment. Suddenly, a pop bottle lifted out of the garbage can beside the path and floated through the air. "I can turn organic material invisible when I touch it, but it doesn't work with large pieces of glass or metal." The bottle floated back into the center of the light, accompanied by the increase in volume of the buzzing.

"Wow!" Edict exclaimed. "You really are invisible! I've never seen an invisible person before. What's your name?"

"Guess," the voice replied.

"I don't know," Edict shrugged. "Can you give me a clue?"

"No," the disembodied voice replied, "My name's Guess, or at least my last name is. My first name's Guy."

"How old are you, Guy?"

"I'm eleven," Guy replied.

"Why won't my plan work?" Loofah demanded.

"You couldn't catch Jack with that rope," Guy said.

"Why not?"

"Because, I tricked Jack," Guy replied. "I buried myself under the straw in my cage. When Jack came by, he couldn't hear me buzz. Naturally, he thought I'd escaped. He opened my cage to make certain, and that's when I grabbed the keys from the door and left!" Guy laughed in spite of himself. "I shut Jack in!"

"Do you still have the keys?" Edict asked. "Perhaps you could let us out!"

"I could," Guy admitted, "but I don't know why I should."

"We'd let you out," Loofah said, "if the tables were turned."

Guy shrugged his shoulders, though neither Edict nor Loofah could see the gesture. "I don't even know the way out of the Zoo yet. This path doesn't lead to the exit, and there aren't any obvious paths that do. I can't take a chance of being stuck here when the sun rises. They'd find me for sure, then."

"We can help you find the way out," Edict promised. "I'm very smart, and even Loofah's a bit brighter than he looks."

"Hey!" Loofah objected. "I thought you said we'd stop insulting each other!"

"Yes," Guy said. "If you two can't get along, I won't let either of you out."

"Sorry Loofah," Edict said. "I'm just having a bit of fun."

"At my expense!" Loofah added.

Edict nodded. "Yeah, at your expense. I won't do it again."

Guy considered in silence for a moment. "Well, I suppose you could help me. I guess three heads are better than one."

"And eight legs are better than two," Loofah interjected.

"If you're a spider, that's absolutely right," Edict agreed.

Loofah and Edict watched as the bottle moved slowly back into the garbage-can. The volume of the buzz diminished appropriately until it disappeared in the darkness behind Edict's cage. The lock clicked, and the door opened.

Edict stepped out of the cage and stretched his arms. "Thanks Guy. That feels a lot less confining."

The lock on Loofah's cage clicked, and soon the three of them stood on the brick pathway. Although neither Loofah nor Edict could see Guy, the constant buzzing sound he made under the lamp informed them of his presence.

"Now, all we have to do is find the exit," Edict informed. "You said the path doesn't lead out?"

"No," Guy shook his invisible head, causing a fluctuation in the buzzing sound. "I've been over it, but I've just been going in circles."

Edict scratched his head. "Let's try it one more time. Perhaps we can question Jack as we go past your old cage."

Loofah nodded in agreement. Guy did not object. Edict began walking down the brick path, followed by the orangutaur and the invisible boy.

"Watch for trails in the dirt by the path," Edict said as they traveled. "It might not be a finished path that leads out of the zoo."

Edict looked for telltale signs of a trail leading away from the brick path as he went along. After some time walking, they approached one of the cages. There wasn't a streetlamp right next to it, so he could not see inside. Edict approached the cage and peered into its dark interior. Not being able to see in the dark like his cousin, he couldn't see very much inside the cage. He thought he saw a glowing, red disk appear and disappear, but wasn't sure if his eyes tricked him for a moment.

"What's this cage for?" Loofah wondered as he came up to peer in with Edict.

Edict shrugged. "I don't know," he admitted. "Can either of you see anything?"

"I don't see anything," Guy replied.

"Do you still have the keys?" Edict asked in the direction of Guy's voice.

"Sure," the invisible boy replied. "Why?"

"Why, I want to investigate naturally."

The keys appeared apparently floating in thin air. "I think this is a waste of time," Guy said in way of filing protest.

"It will only take a minute," Edict assured. Moving around to the back of the cage, he inserted the key in the lock and walked inside. He could make out the form of Loofah outside the front of the cage. "I wish I had a flashlight," he muttered.

Edict peered into the darkest corner. A pair of glowing, red eyes suddenly flashed at him. He fell against the bars and onto the straw covered concrete floor. He quickly stumbled out of the cage and onto the grass. The large, glowing orbs appeared in the open doorway.

The moon lit the form of a tall creature with wings like a moth. Its glowing eyes appeared to be in its chest, as it seemed to have no separate head or arms aside from the wings. A fine, grey fur covered its body. The imposing figure seemed curious about Edict's identity.

"Mothman," Edict whispered.

Loofah rushed around the corner. "What's going on, Edict?" The orangutaur halted as he saw the frightening figure approaching Edict. "Oh."

The Mothman turned to Loofah, and let out an inhuman, high-pitched squeal. Apparently, Loofah had surprised it. The orangutaur used the moment to run next to Edict and offered his hand. "Come on!" Loofah said.

Edict grasped Loofah's hand and swung upon the orangutaur's back. The Mothman moved toward them as Loofah began to run as fast as his horse-legs would carry him and his burden. Loofah rushed over the grass field behind the cage.

The Mothman took a few running steps to assist in launching itself into the air. It wildly flapped its wings as it pursued Edict and Loofah.

Luckily, Edict had honed his equestrian skills when his parents allowed him take horseback riding classes. Still, riding on Loofah proved different and more difficult than a regular horse. Edict held onto the orangutaur's thick back hair.

"What about Guy?" Edict asked as he rode.

Loofah shrugged. "He'll be fine. He's invisible, and inaudible as long as he stays in the dark."

A high-pitched squeal reminded the pair that the Mothman hunted them. Edict looked back to see it flying very close behind, despite Loofah's high rate of speed.

"Faster!" Edict exclaimed. "Faster!"

"I would go faster without you!" Loofah reminded.

Edict decided to cease his complaints. "It will catch up to you with or without me," he explained. "We need a plan, and we need it fast!"

"I've got a plan," Loofah said with a smile.

Edict groaned. "It's not like your last one, I hope."

"No, this one's different. We're not trying to escape from a cage. This plan's for escaping a giant moth-creature."

The Mothman squealed again. Edict turned to see the creature coming uncomfortably close. "Any time you want to try your plan before the Mothman captures us would be good."

"I'm heading that way."

"Which way?" Edict could not see why Loofah headed for a small knoll until they reached the top. "Oh, no," he said. "This is a bad idea."

A large, carnivorous dinosaur reared its head as they topped the knoll. "Hold on!" Loofah shouted and headed right for the tyrannosaurus rex.

"Don't!" Edict objected too late.

The dinosaur pulled its head back to take a strike at the orangutaur and its rider, but Loofah sped up and rushed between the tyrannosaur's feet.

'Good thing the scientists were wrong when they thought the tyrannosaur's pulled their tails on the ground,' Edict thought, 'or we'd run right into it.'

The tyrannosaur began to turn and follow the prey that had run between its legs. As it did so, the Mothman came over the rise and crashed right into the dinosaur with a surprised squeal. The impact angered the dinosaur. It turned its attention to the Mothman, which recovered and flew quickly away. The tyrannosaur chased after it.

"Whew!" Loofah laughed. "That was close!"

Edict frowned. "Too close. That was reckless and dangerous!"

Loofah turned his head to nod and smile. "More important," the orangutaur replied, "it was fun!"

Edict attempted to retain his anger, but soon a smile crept across his face. "It was fun," he admitted. "Perhaps we should try again?"

Loofah shook his head. "Fun is fun, but we need to find Guy and leave the zoo."

"I'm here!" Guy said as he huffed and puffed like the sound of a steam engine. He must have run the distance. "Say," Guy said, "what are all these flags in the ground?"

Loofah shrugged. "Beats me senseless with a stick," the orangutaur said.

"They're hole markers," Edict informed. "We're on a golf-course."

"Well, that doesn't help us at all," Guy put in. "We still need to get out of the zoo."

Mothman

CHAPTER VIII
THE TOCSIN COUSINS REUNITE

The darkness of night still ruled when Eerey awoke. She looked around the sand trap. Both the worm and Pen had left. She stood to her feet and held her head. Even though the worm had not given her a lethal blow from the invisible death-force, it still delivered quite a shock to her system.

Eerey headed for the nearest edge of the sand trap. The next Mongolian death worm she ran across might not be as gracious. Looking around the golf course, she saw a large tyrannosaurus rex towering high over the golf flags. 'Great,' she thought. 'Either be shocked by Mongolian death worms or be eaten by a dinosaur.'

Just as she considered her options, a large and weird creature flew into the dinosaur. 'A mothman,' Eerey thought to herself. The dinosaur snapped at it with its jaws and began to chase it across the golf course. The two creatures headed for the eighteenth hole, which was fine with Eerey as she stood near the first.

Eerey saw something else on top of the knoll. From the distance, it looked like a small centaur with a rider on its back. Although she could not make out the features of either figure, she decided to take a cautious closer look. She moved across the golf course toward them.

As she neared, she recognized her cousin astride a strange looking centaur with orangutan features for its torso and head.

"Edict!" she shouted and waved her arms. "Edict! Over here!"

Edict, Guy, and Loofah turned their heads to look in the direction of the voice. They saw a white form moving toward them but could not make it out.

"Who's that?" Loofah wanted to know.

"Edict shrugged. "Beats me."

Eerey yelled again. "Edict! It's me, Eerey!"

"What's Eerie?" Loofah asked.

"I don't know," Edict responded. "But for some reason, I think 'Edict' is my name. Maybe I've met her before?"

"Let's go check it out," Guy said.

"Might as well," Loofah replied with a shrug. They could now make out the white figure belonged to a young girl. They walked toward her as she ran toward them.

Edict's band stopped, as did Eerey. They stood within a few yards of each other. "Edict!" Eerey shouted as she continued to move toward them. "It's me, your cousin Eerey!"

"Don't you mean my eerie cousin?" Edict asked as she flung her arms around his neck.

Eerey did not pay attention to the comment as she held Edict tightly around the neck. "Your making quite a burden of yourselves," Loofah interjected. "In other words, Edict, or whatever your name is-get off my back!"

"He's right, of course," Edict said as Eerey let go long enough for him to dismount. Eerey smiled at him once he was on the ground. "What's your name, anyway?"

Eerey frowned. "I told you-I'm Eerey, Edict. stop playing around. I've come to rescue you!"

Edict's eyes narrowed. "So, you're the one who called me a troglodyte in that letter and got me into this mess."

Eerey looked at Edict, and saw that he really did not remember. She looked at her shiny, black shoes. "Yes, I did," she said. "I've come to rectify the problem."

"Aren't you going to introduce us?" Guy's disembodied voice interrupted the reunion.

"Oh, yes. Eerey," Edict said tenuously, "these are my friends, Loofah the orangutaur, and Guy the invisible boy."

"Pleased to meet you," Eerey assured. "Why do they call you the invisible boy, Guy?"

"For obvious reasons," Guy responded, then added, "It's because I'm invisible!"

"You are?" Eerey asked, looking right at Guy. "You're a bit transparent, but clearly not invisible!"

"You...you can see me?" Guy stammered.

"Of course I can see you."

"Oh, yes, Edict broke in, "I think I remember now. My cousin has uncanny eyesight in the dark. Perhaps it extends to invisible things as well."

Eerey's eyes narrowed as she pointed them at Edict. "So, you do remember me."

Edict shook his head. "No, I just remember I had a cousin that could see in the dark."

"I've never met anyone who could see me!" Guy said with admiration. "What color jacket am I wearing?"

Eerey laughed. "You don't have to try to trick me. You're not wearing a jacket. You're wearing a t-shirt with a picture of Claude Rains."

"Claude Rains?" Edict repeated. "Why him?"

Guy stood silent for a moment before replying. "Claude Rains played *The Invisible Man* in the movie," he said finally. "He's my hero."

"So you *are* wearing that t-shirt," Loofah decided to believe Eerey could see Guy after all..

Eerey nodded. "Yes, and a pair of blue jeans."

"Is that what you're wearing, Guy?" Edict asked.

"Yes," Guy replid. "Your cousin can really see me!"

Scanning the area with her eyes, Eerey cut the conversation short. "We need to get moving. That dinosaur and that mothman might return at any time."

"She's right," Loofah agreed. "We still need to find our way out of the zoo, too."

Eerey shook her head. "I don't think we'll be able to get out of here until we free Mister Cryptic."

"Free Mister Cryptic? Are you crazy?" Edict objected. "He's the one that put me in the cage in the first place!"

"That wasn't Mister Cryptic," Eerey replied. "Pen's a doppelganger."

Loofah pulled at his chin with his long fingers. "What's a doppelganger?"

"A doppelganger is a creature that shape-shifts to look like any human or animal it wants to look like," Edict offered.

"Where's the real Mister Cryptic then?" Guy asked.

"Imprisoned somewhere in the zoo, I imagine," Eerey surmised. "We've got to find him. He might be the only one who can stop Pen and show us the way to go home. Maybe he can restore Edict's memory as well."

Edict turned to Guy. "Guy, did you check all the cages on the path?"

"Why should I?" Guy shrugged. "I just wanted out, not to take a tour of the zoo."

"Perhaps Mister Cryptic's being kept in one of the cages!" Eerey suggested. "The first thing we need to do is check all the cages. "Which way are they?"

Guy pointed toward a row of trees. "They're that way."

Neither Loofah nor Edict could see the gesture, but Eerey understood. "Thanks, Guy," she said and started walking. The three followed her.

"Say, Loofah…" Edict started, but Loofah interrupted him.

"Not if your life depended on it," the orangutaur said as he used his long arms to reach back and rub the top of the horse part of his body. "You can't have a horsy-back ride. My spine's killing me."

Guy Guess (invisible boy)

CHAPTER IX
INSPECTING THE CRYPTIC CAGES

The group returned to the brick path and began going through the cages. Most of the cages had streetlamps lighting the path. The first they came upon held a familiar sight.

Edict smiled at the display. "How're you doing Jack?"

The zookeeper in the blue jumpsuit and cap came to the front of the cage and held onto the bars. He leered at Edict. "How'd you get out?"

Edict walked over to the cart of fresh fruits and vegetables Jack had abandoned to check on the invisible boy. He picked up a vegetable. "Do you want a rutabaga, Jack?" Edict taunted.

Jack's expression turned angry. "Let me out of here!"

"Well, you'll want one when you get hungry," Edict jabbed.

"Stop it, Edict," Eerey said. "This doesn't help us at all."

"It's helping me feel better," Edict muttered.

"Jack," Eerey addressed the man in the cage. "If we let you out, will you tell us where the real Mister Cryptic is?"

Jack grasped the bars and stared at the strange band for a minute. Finally, he began to laugh. "Mister Cryptic's indisposed!" "You could say he's buried under his work, or you could say he has the weight of the world on his shoulders! I'll relay the message that you want to see him!" With that, Jack continued with his infuriating laugh.

"Come on Eerey," Edict said. "He's not going to tell us anything."

Jack's laughter followed them as they continued down the path. It died out after a while.

Some time after the four departed, a figure approached Jack laughing in his cage. "I see you have not been fulfilling your duties," Pen said as he slipped from the darkness into the light. "Or are you having a laugh with the invisible boy?"

Jack moved back a bit at seeing Pen. "Mister Cryptic, the

invisible boy tricked me and escaped. The orangutaur and that new talking troglodyte Edict have escaped too."

"Escaped?" Pen frowned. "You allowed them to get out? I have only had them less than a week!"

Jack nodded. "I know, but they got out in less than a week. Mister Cryptic never kept the creatures in cages."

"I am Mister Cryptic!" Pen admonished. He sighed. "Apparently, intelligence doesn't always extend to human animals. Which way did they go?"

"The three of them went up the path."

"The three of them?" Pen repeated. "Was the invisible boy with them as well?"

Jack shook his head. "I didn't see him. They had some girl with them."

"A girl? What was her name?"

"I didn't hear a name," Jack admitted. "That troglodyte said she was eerie, though."

"Eerey, you buffoon," Pen raged, "is the little girl's name!"

"That's an odd name," Jack said, rubbing his chin.

"It's an odd name for an odd little girl," Pen said, "it's an odder name for a little girl who's supposed to be dead."

"Dead!" Jack exclaimed. "No wonder they call her eerie."

"It's amazing you can even remember to breathe," Pen replied. "I should never have put you in charge of watching out for the displays. A dodo bird could outwit you!"

"The dodo birds don't usually try to escape," Jack reminded. "Besides, I caught them again."

Pen walked away from Jack's cage in disgust.

"Hey!" Jack said. "Aren't you going to let me out?"

"An orangutaur, a troglodyte and an invisible boy figured out how to escape," Pen said over his shoulder. "I'll assume you can figure it out."

Pen walked out of the light. He removed an ornate whistle from his pocket and blew into it. In a few moments, a bevy of giant bats arrived through the trees. Their shrieks filled the air as they created a tornado of batwings and fur around Pen.

"Children of the night," he addressed the bats, "you must dispose of some problem creatures."

Pen removed from his jacket pocket Eerey's letter. He flapped it about above his head to let the bats' sensitive noses pick up Eerey and Edict's particular scents. This being finished, the bats flew along the path toward the direction the four escapees had traveled.

Eerey, Edict, Guy and Loofah checked through many interesting, uninteresting, and empty cages without discovering the whereabouts of the authentic Mr. Cryptic.

In one section of the zoo they met with all sorts of large cats the size of tigers and lions, but quite different from either in many respects. For example, one of the large cats had six toes on each paw and bright-blue fur. Another had forest-green and brown fur to serve as camouflage for the jungle. Unfortunately, the animals in that section could not, or would not, speak.

The party continued on to the next section of cages. Suddenly, Edict stopped. The other three also stopped and looked at him.

"Do you hear that?" Edict asked.

Eerey looked around for the origin of Edict's concern.

"Hear what?"

"It's a high-pitched sound," Edict responded. He shrugged after further consideration. "I don't know where it's coming from."

"I hear it now," Eerey whispered. "It's getting louder." She scanned the darkness with her keen vision.

"Bats," Loofah said as he looked about.

"I'm not crazy!" Eerey objected.

"No," Loofah replied. "You're not bats. That sound is coming from bats."

"Vampire bats!" Guy exclaimed loudly.

"Hush," Edict said.

"But I don't like bats," the invisible boy quietly informed. "I can stay invisible, but bats don't see with their eyes. I'm completely vulnerable to their sensitive hearing directed by their sonic sounds."

"We're all vulnerable," Eerey reminded. "You're only in the same boat as everyone else."

"We need to hide," Edict said, "quickly!"

The group ran for a nearby grove of trees by the path and hid. Soon, the gigantic bats appeared over the trail, the light from the lamps casting their long, black shadows on the red bricks. Their sound equaled their enormous size, and soon a cacophony of high-pitched squeals filled the entire area.

The oversized bats flitted between the trees, still following the Eerey and Edict's scent. The screeching noises painfully invaded Eerey's ears. She held her hands over them, but made no sound in reply.

Eerey felt a pair of hands on her shoulders accompanied by a slight buzzing. She turned to see Guy's frightened face. She took her hands off her ears. "What if they find us?" he whispered just loud enough so only she could hear.

Eerey shook her head. "I suspect it would not be good," she whispered in reply. She started to return her hands to her ears, when she saw her fingers and palms retained a translucent appearance. "Guy," she said, "why are you buzzing?"

Guy shrugged. "I buzz in the light," he said.

"It's pitch-black right now," Eerey informed. "You've made me invisible too. Take your hands off my shoulders for a moment," she said.

Guy removed his hands and the buzzing stopped. Eerey's mind worked quickly. "I think we can get rid of the bats. Follow me."

Guy obediently followed Eerey as she moved toward Loofah. She had Loofah follow her to Edict and quietly instructed them all to follow her back to the path.

The bats hunted the scent as the four moved out of the grove. "Let's head for the lamps," Eerey said, this time at a normal volume. She broke out into a run as her three companions imitated her.

Guy caught up with Eerey and ran beside her. "I'm going to

start buzzing in the light," he protested.

"I know," Eerey replied as she continued running.

Under the full blast of the streetlamp, Guy buzzed loudly. "Now they're going to find us for sure!" he shouted.

Eerey nodded her head and grabbed onto his hand. Guy's buzzing increased. "Where's Eerey?" Edict asked as she disappeared. He felt Eerey's invisible hand grasp his. He looked at his hand and watched it disappear. "Cool!" he commented loudly.

"Grab Loofah's hand!" Eerey shouted over Guy's now deafening buzz. Edict did as instructed as Guy grasped Loofah's other hand. The orangutaur became invisible as the four created a ring of invisibility.

"Now we're all invisible!" Eerey yelled.

"Bats don't need their sight!" Loofah reminded.

"I know!" Eerey replied. "They do need their ears!"

By the time the bats caught up with the quintet, the buzzing noise became quite unbearable for them. The bats began fluttering about in confusion as the noise disrupted their radar sense. They bumped into the light pole like moths to a flame. They could not navigate inside the confusing buzz. Although they still smelled their prey, the buzzing made it impossible for them to seek them out with their radar.

"It's working!" Guy shouted.

"They are starting to leave!" Edict agreed. The bats flew away, one by one, as they tired of the painful sound. In a few moments, all the bats abandoned the hunt and their prey.

Eerey let go of Guy's hand and became visible once more. "We can keep going," she said. "We need to find Mister Cryptic."

Asentizio (leader of the Morlocks)

CHAPTER X
THE DOOR IN THE BLACK WALL

"Where we should begin searching?" Edict queried. He moved to the side of the path to examine a dodo bird inside a cage and rest for a moment. "I mean, we have no idea where Mister Cryptic might be."

"We must keep going," Eerey insisted as she pulled on Edict's sleeve. "If we don't find Mister Cryptic, Pen will catch up to us. Then it will be too late."

"My hooves are tired," Loofah complained.

"That can't be helped right now," Eerey said. "We can rest after we've escaped the zoo."

"Easy for you to say," Loofah remarked. "You don't have hooves."

"You have an extra pair of feet the rest of us don't," Edict reminded.

"Yes," Loofah agreed. "but you haven't been carrying anybody on your back, either."

Edict started to reply when Eerey interrupted the conversation. "Look!" she exclaimed and pointed up the path. Even in the moonlit dimness, the party could see a metal door set into an irregular cliff of shiny, black rock.

Guy's eyes widened. "What? Is that a wall?"

Eerey nodded. "It surrounds the entire Cryptoid Zoo. That is, if Pen did not lie to me about that."

Edict shrugged. "There's no reason to expect he lied. There's no reason to suspect he told you the truth, either. Maybe Mister Cryptic is behind that door," he suggested.

Lost in thought, Eerey tried to remember what Jack had said about Mr. Cryptic. "Jack said Mister Cryptic was buried under his work," she mused. "That's an odd thing to say."

"Let's see what's behind the door," Edict suggested. He

walked up to the door and pulled on the handle. He let go and turned to his companions. "It's locked."

"It's not locked," Guy replied. "It's not there."

"What are you talking about?" Edict asked. "I can see it!"

Eerey shook her head. "Guy's right, it isn't there. I'm surprised I didn't see it before."

"Well, I see it," Loofah assured. "You're talking crazy."

"It's not easy to see through the invisible against a black wall," Eerey said. "Guy can see through the invisible, being invisible himself, and I've trained myself to see what cannot be readily seen."

Guy nodded, but only Eerey could see him nod. "That's true. I believe we've just been hypnotized to see the door," he suggested.

"It's worse if it's really not there," Edict said. "If our minds think it's there and locked, there's no way to get past it. We've got to break the hypnotic spell, but how?"

"We might not have to," Guy suggested. "I think Loofah's right, the door is there after all."

"What?" Eerey and Edict asked in unison.

"Thank you," Loofah grinned. "Of course, I'm right. An orangutaur's always right."

"I think I still have a key in my pocket," Guy went on. "I took it from Jack. Here it is, Loofah."

Loofah watched as a key appeared in the diffused moonlight. "Thank you," he said as he took the key. He placed the key in the lock and turned it. He heard it click, and pulled the door open by the handle. "There! It's open now."

As Loofah opened the door, it began to fade until it disappeared. It left in its place a door-sized hole with a rock staircase descending into darkness. The key in Loofah's hand likewise vanished. "Hey!" the orangutaur exclaimed. "That's impossible!"

Eerey nodded. "Your conviction that the door was real allowed Guy to give you a key that you also thought was real. Through your belief, you have done the impossible and gone through a door that doesn't exist."

"If the door didn't exist," Loofah pondered quietly, "then I was wrong."

"Cheer up, old chap!" Edict replied. "We couldn't have gotten past the door if you weren't so wrong! In that way, you were both right and wrong at the same time!"

Loofah smiled slightly. "I guess you're right. Sometimes, being wrong can be a good thing."

"Right!" Edict agreed.

Loofah smiled as Eerey began descending the steps. The others followed her into the darkness. "I wish we had a flashlight," Eerey said quietly as she shuddered. "It's even too dark for me to see. I don't like it."

The invisible boy followed Eerey down the stairway. "I can't see anything either," Guy admitted. "I can't even see myself in this!"

"Maybe we should go back," Loofah suggested from the back of the line.

"Hush," Edict replied. "If we can't see, we would do well to use our other senses."

"Other senses?" Guy asked.

None of them saw Eerey nod, but she did so. "Yes," she agreed. "We have at least five. Loofah's sense of smell should be particularly acute, for example."

"He's not that cute," Edict chuckled.

"Knock it off," Loofah grumbled. "It's not smart to insult someone right behind you."

Edict shrugged. "Let's feel our way along the walls," he suggested. "Loofah, if you smell anything unusual, let us know. I can hear fairly well, so I'll listen for things."

"What about our sense of taste?" Guy asked.

"I doubt we'll find anything that requires tasting," Eerey replied.

"If we do, I'll taste it," Guy volunteered.

They continued through the enveloping darkness in silence. The warm, humid air seemed to be the very substance of shadow.

Every slight and unidentifiable sound added to the quartet's growing fears.

Eerey began to count aloud. "235, 236," she said.

"What are you doing?" Edict asked.

"I'm counting the stairs," she replied. "It may be helpful later."

Edict doubted it would ever be of use, but he said nothing.

They occasionally misjudged their feet and stumbled. "The air is getting warmer," Edict noted.

"Yes," Loofah agreed, "and we've been going down these steps for an awfully long time."

Eerey suddenly stopped counting and moving. "The stairs have ended," she said. "It's level here."

Edict stepped onto the flat surface. "Whew! I thought that stairwell would never end."

"We must have gone down for miles," Loofah agreed.

"I don't think so," Eerey replied. "There are 1576 stairs total. I think that's how many stairs there are in the Empire State Building, and that's not a mile high. Darkness distorts our sense of time and distance."

"Isn't the sense of time a sixth sense?" Guy asked.

"Probably," Eerey guessed.

The familiar act of conversation comforted them for a moment. A deep and repeating echo filled the air, suggesting a large area. The moment of comfort passed as quickly as it had arrived when multiple torches of fire appeared in the darkness. The fires flickered off the walls and between the stalactites and stalagmites of a vast cavern. The light revealed the ceiling of the cavern, about twenty-two feet from the floor. Growling noises accompanied the flickering flames. Tall, humanoid figures carrying torches approached the travelers. The four companions moved closer together.

"Who's that?" Eerey asked, trying to adjust her eyes to the bright light after spending so much time in utter darkness. She retrieved her mother's sunglasses and returned them to her face.

The growling grew louder as the figures surrounded them.

Loofah's eyes adjusted first to the torchlight. "Troglodytes!" he exclaimed.

"No," Edict shook his head as he identified the creatures, "Morlocks." The creatures' tiny, dark eyes reflected the fires of their torches. Their long, sharp teeth displayed threatening grimaces. Long and thick black hair covered their bodies. Grayish skin displayed itself beneath the hair. Their arms and fingers were exceptionally long. Their legs remained bent at all times, as if in preparation to leap to attack at any moment.

Eerey looked for the stairwell they had descended. Only smooth walls of obsidian greeted her searching eyes. The passage had disappeared, and any chance of escape that way became impossible.

"I don't think they are happy to see us," Guy mentioned.

"Don't worry," Edict replied. "At least they can't see you. You're invisible."

"Yeah," Loofah agreed. "Why aren't you buzzing?"

"The light isn't bright enough to make me buzz," Guy replied.

"Well, stop your mouth from buzzing," Edict quipped. "They'll find you if you don't quit talking."

Guy took Edict's advice and fell silent. The Morlocks moved closer to the group as Guy slipped away unseen.

"This is it," Loofah informed.

"As long as you can say it's over," Eerey reminded, "it's not over."

A Morlock grabbed Eerey's arms and restrained them. She kicked at him until another Morlock grabbed her feet and held them in one of his large hands. Another leapt onto Loofah's back and held his arms still. The orangutaur attempted to buck the creature off like a horse, but two other Morlocks quickly bound his legs with some green vines and Loofah fell to the ground.

A group of Morlocks surrounded Edict and started to sniff at his head. They grabbed his arms and held them. They continued to pull roughly at the hair on his head and face.

"Cut that out!" Edict protested, but the Morlocks merely

growled and continued their inspection. When they completed their survey, they let go of Edict's arms. A tall Morlock carrying a staff approached the scene, wearing a long robe with designs of red and black outlined with gold thread.

"It's the Golden 'Lock!" one of the Morlocks informed the staff-bearer.

Loofah grumbled. "Does every creature in this zoo talk?"

"I'm not a Morlock," Edict protested.

The Morlock with the staff addressed Edict directly. "Your coming has been foretold from time before memory. It has been written a Morlock with hair of light will come to restore us to the Great Light. It is you we have awaited!" The tall Morlock gracefully bowed toward Edict while the other Morlocks about him fell to the ground in worship.

Edict planned in his head quickly. "If that's true," he said to the Morlock, "you will release my friends at once!"

The tall Morlock nodded his head to Loofah and Eerey's captors, and they released the pair with stumbling apologies. "My name is Asentzio," the tall Morlock introduced himself. "I am the leader of the Morlocks. That is, until you arrived."

Edict waved his hands dismissively. "I am not here to take your job away. I am here only to restore the Morlocks to the Great Light." He looked at the Morlocks bowing to him. "Arise. I cannot lead you to the Great Light when you face the darkness of the ground."

His words surprised Eerey. He certainly thought well on his feet. She watched as the Morlocks stood up. "Now what?" she whispered to Edict.

Edict failed to reply. Instead, he spoke to Asentzio. "Explain the plight of the Morlocks to me."

"Long ago," Asentzio began, "Morlocks lived beneath the bright and loving beams of the shining white orb. It gave sustenance and comfort. When the orb disappeared and the burning orb replaced it, we always returned into the moderate warmth of this cave. We wish to bask in the orb's light again, but an evil warlock has hidden the path to the surface for a great, long time."

"How long ago was that?" Eerey broke in, unable to hide her curiosity.

Asentzio place rubbed his chin with his hand and looked upward. Finally, he had an answer. "Six full revolutions of the shining white orb," he replied.

"That's not so long ago!" Loofah protested. "That's only six months or so!"

"Be quiet!" Edict shushed. "Remember, darkness distorts one's sense of time. A few months can seem like an eternity." He continued speaking to Asentzio; "What was this warlock's name?"

"Pendragon," Asentzio replied.

"Pen!" Eerey exclaimed.

Asentzio nodded. "That was what the warlock called himself. He deceived us into thinking he was Mister Cryptic. By the time the worms informed us, we had become trapped down here."

"You speak to worms?" Loofah asked.

"No," Asentzio shook his head. "We listen to the worms; they speak to us. If we listen to what nature says, we can live in harmony."

"Listen to me then," Edict said. "We will find another way out of here. We will return to show you the way to the light. However, the four of us must make the journey alone."

"Four?" Asentizio queried. His dark eyes narrowed. "Have you been deceiving us while another lurks in the darkness? No Morlock would lie to his own kind!"

Edict shook his head. "I'm not lying, and I told you I'm not a Morlock."

Edict's speech did not help the party. Asentzio's brow fell into a frightening expression. "Not a Morlock?" he growled. "It is another trick by the wizard Pendragon!" he shouted. "He has taken this form to trick us!"

The Morlocks began to howl loudly as they approached the group. Mere moments before the creatures closed around them,

Edict disappeared before their eyes. The sight took the Morlocks back for a moment, but another shouted, "It is a warlock's trick!"

The Morlocks rushed Eerey and Loofah, but they too disappeared. The Morlocks swung their arms about wildly, but the invisible four slid past the blind gropes of the Morlocks and escaped into the cavern's darkness.

Giant Chameleon Crocodile

CHAPTER XI
THE UNDERGROUND RAINBOW

The travelers came across several caves in the walls of the vast cavern. The Morlocks began to extend their search of the area as they sniffed and groped the warm air. Their howls became quite unnerving.

"Which cave should we take?" Loofah asked quietly.

The darkness hid Eerey's shrug. "Since we have no idea where these caverns go, it really doesn't matter. Escaping is our first priority."

This suggestion seemed reasonable. As the Morlocks continued to search, Guy led his companions into one of the small caves heading away from the enormous cavern.

Soon, darkness enveloped the party. They traveled for long minutes in silence holding hands.

"Can you see anything, Eerey?" Edict whispered as they stumbled along the cavern.

"There's light up ahead," Eerey replied. "I've been able to see it for a while, but it's still a long way off."

"Good," Loofah broke in. "I don't care for this darkness."

They continued walking until Edict exclaimed, "I can see it now!"

"Shhh!" Eerey said. "We'll be there in a minute, but we don't want the Morlocks to hear us!"

"I don't think we were followed," Guy offered.

"The Morlocks didn't follow us," Loofah assured. He crinkled his nose in the darkness. "Their smell is unmistakable!"

"We're almost there," Eerey said. "The light is moving. Guy, perhaps you can go ahead?"

"Sure." Guy let go of Eerey's hand. The invisible boy traveled toward the multi-colored light pouring around a corner in the cavern. He maneuvered around the stalagmites pushing upward and the stalactites hanging from the ceiling. He looked around the corner into another cave. "Come on," he yelled back. "It's just a river."

Loofah huffed at the news. "At least we know we won't die of thirst."

The others joined Guy and looked into the cave. A clear river flowed tranquilly through it. The water reflected the light produced by colonies of luminescent lichen. The colonies were different colors, each glowing brightly. The humidity from the water created a rainbow effect.

"It's beautiful," Edict said as his eyes drank the sight of the underground rainbow.

Eerey nodded her agreement. "It's a natural light show!"

The four stood on the shore looking at the fantastic display of light for a moment, until Loofah interrupted them. "We should get wading. That is, if we've decided to continue going this way."

Edict nodded. "We should wade upstream. It should lead somewhere."

"Any way you go leads to somewhere," Loofah reminded. "We don't want to go somewhere. We need to find Mister Cryptic, remember?"

"Yeah, I remember," Edict replied. "If we go upstream, we could find the source of the water, and maybe a way out. Once we know that, we can leave if we do find Mister Cryptic." He added, "We should take off our shoes and carry them."

"Don't joke," the orangutaur said. "My shoes are nailed on. How deep is it, anyway?"

"You can see the bottom," Eerey replied as she sat down to take off her shoes. "The water's clear, but you can't always tell how deep it is by looking." She tested the water with one of her bare toes, "and it's warm, too." She held her up the bottom of her dress and stepped in. The water came up to her knees.

Edict and Guy sat down to take their shoes off. Edict didn't bother rolling his pants up as he stepped in. "It feels nice!"

"Yeah," Loofah agreed as he followed. "Dogface is right, it does feel good."

Edict laughed at Loofah's 'dogface' comment.

"Can we put our shoes in your pack?" Guy asked Eerey. He started to unzip the zipper without waiting for an answer. Eightball stuck his feet out of the pack.

"Whoa!" Guy yelled as he fell backwards into the river.

"What the heck is that?" Loofah asked.

Eerey zipped the backpack up again. "That's Eightball," she informed. "He's my pet."

"Your pet?" Guy asked. "You keep a giant spider for a pet?"

Eerey shook her head. "He's not all that big. He only weighs about eight pounds."

"That's about eight pounds too big for me!" Loofah said with a shudder. "Get rid of that thing!"

"No way!" Eerey growled.

Edict shook his head at Loofah. "She'll never get rid of it," he said. "You might as well give it up."

"I'm not walking behind her!" Loofah assured.

"I'll walk behind you," Eerey replied. "Though, I don't know why you'd want a giant spider at your back if you dislike it so much."

Loofah replied with a big splash as he leapt behind Eerey. "I'll keep an eye on it," he assured.

After the initial shock, Guy's curiosity grew. "That's your pet?" he asked as he waded upstream beside Eerey. The smooth stones on their feet and warm water on their legs felt good after all the walking they had done.

"More than a pet," Eerey replied. "He's my friend."

"Some kind of a Charlotte's Web thing, eh?" Loofah teased as he followed Eerey and Guy.

Edict, walking beside Loofah, pushed at the orangutaur's arm. "Leave her alone, Loofah," he said. "You're already starting to smell like a wet horse as it is without being annoying!"

"Smell who's talking," Loofah replied. "You already stink like a wet dog!"

"Let's practice some civility," Eerey suggested. "This is hard enough without your incessant bickering."

As they traveled around a bend in the cavern, they saw the source of the water. The mouth of the river flowed from a large underground lake. The same colonies of lichen that illuminated the river lit the lake and caused a larger rainbow effect in the enormous cavern. A shore of black, glassy sand started in the middle of the grotto.

"I guess this is where the river comes from," Guy ventured.

Eerey nodded. "Yes. The water comes into the lake from that waterfall over there." She pointed across the cavern to where water fell from the ceiling. She continued; "We can't climb to where the water comes in. It's too dangerous. There's light shining from behind the waterfall, so the cavern must continue that way."

"How are we going to get across the lake?" Loofah asked.

Edict peered into the transparent water of the lake. "It doesn't look much deeper than the river. We could wade to the shore in the middle."

"Oh," Loofah said. "That's good if I don't want to be dry again."

The group began wading across the water. After they were about twenty feet from shore, Guy whispered harshly, "Stop!"

His companions stopped and looked in the direction of the invisible boy's voice. "Why?" Edict whispered.

"Because we're not alone," Guy replied.

Loofah looked around. "I don't see anything," he said aloud.

"Shush!" Guy demanded. "You can't see it."

"Can you?" Edict asked, peering around.

"No," Guy admitted. "I can't see it, but I know it's here."

"What's here?" Loofah wanted to know.

"I don't know. You can probably smell it if you'll try."

Flaring his nostrils wide, Loofah sniffed the air. His eyes grew wide. "You're right!" he huffed.

"What do you smell?" Eerey asked quietly.

"It's a crocodile!" Loofah replied. "But why can't we see it?"

Eerey took off her backpack and unzipped it. She rummaged around, past the candy bars, comics, and the huge spider. Finally, she retrieved Mr. Cryptic's book. After replacing her pack, she flipped through the pages. She stopped on a page, and began to read; "It's probably a *Sarcosuchus imperator,* a giant prehistoric crocodile."

"Prehistoric means extinct!" Loofah objected.

Eerey shook her head. "Prehistoric just means it's ancient, not extinct. Mister Cryptic says the giant crocodile might have survived by having unusual abilities."

"What unusual abilities?" Loofah snorted.

Eerey read further. "Mister Cryptic suggests they could have been chameleons. They might be able to take on the color of their surroundings."

"So that's why we can't see it," Edict interjected. "It blends in too well."

While Edict said this, something large splashed into the lake by the waterfalls. The party could see a wake approach them in the water, but they could not see what created it.

"Quick!" Eerey shouted. "Get to the shore!"

"How big did you say this thing was?" Loofah asked as he rushed toward the shore.

"The book says they can get up to forty feet long," Eerey replied.

"Well, that's comforting at least," Edict said with a hint of sarcasm. "The giant crocodile we can't see chasing us, is not much bigger than a large school bus."

"This is no time to wax poetic," Eerey reminded. "Besides, it's not very good poetry, either."

"Yes," Edict agreed, "but it may be the last chance I get to make up bad poetry."

"Really you two," Loofah broke in. "Isn't it enough having an enormous monster after us? It doesn't seem fair that it's one we can't see as well."

"Of course, we can see him," Guy reminded. "He might be camouflaged, but he's not invisible."

"Well, I can't see him," Loofah protested.

"Maybe you're not looking hard enough."

"That's true," Eerey broke in. "When I can't see something in the dark, it's usually because I don't know where to look."

"Probably in front of that wake in the water," Edict suggested.

The wake meandered lazily around the lake. The crocodile waited for an opportune moment.

"I think it's stalking us," Loofah suggested.

"It will catch us if we aren't able to see it," Guy reminded. "Concentrate on the front of the wake. Once we see it, it will seem obvious."

The four concentrated on the front of the wake, trying to anticipate where it would go next. They waited for long minutes trying to discern the crocodile's shape. Finally, Loofah exclaimed, "I see it!" He pointed at the water in front of the wake. Now that he saw it, it seemed everyone saw it at once.

"I see it too," Eerey said. "Can everybody see it?"

Guy and Edict nodded.

Eerey offered a cautious smile. "Well, that's part of the problem solved. Now we need to figure out how to get past it."

"We'll need to distract it," Guy suggested. "I can stay here and splash around in the water."

"You'll get eaten," Edict reminded.

"No. I'll stop when he gets close," Guy promised. "He can't see me if I'm not moving."

"Crocodiles use their sense of smell more than their eyesight," Loofah reminded. "He'd follow the smell more than the movement in the water." The orangutaur shrugged. "I'll stay here and splash in the water while you guys sneak away."

"Why you?" Eerey asked.

"I smell the worst," Loofah admitted. "Maybe I can keep the croc interested in me while you three go through the waterfall. Besides, I'm the fastest here, and I have the best chance of outrunning it."

"You might smell worse," Edict agreed, "but what if you can't outrun it?"

Loofah shrugged. "I'll figure something out." With that, the orangutaur jumped in the water and began wildly thrashing about. The wake began to move in the orangutaur's direction.

"Loofah!" Edict shouted. "Get back here!"

Loofah ignored Edict. "Come on," Eerey urged. "We've got to go now!"

The three left Loofah splashing in the water. Eerey took Edict's hand and Guy's as well. The three disappeared and began sneaking quietly down the shore. The wake continued toward Loofah. Loofah watched the enormous, multi-colored camouflaged crocodile swim toward him with amazing speed. He began to head toward the shore, but stopped and watched.

"It's not following me!" Loofah shouted to the others. "It smells Edict instead!"

Sure enough, the crocodile swam directly toward the three invisible youths on the shore.

Edict saw the crocodile headed toward them. "Run!" he shouted. Guy let go of Edict and Eerey's hands so they could run faster. The crocodile gained on them quickly, but they were nearly at the waterfall. They had to outrun the beast if they wanted to survive.

Giant Bats

CHAPTER XII
THROUGH A GLASS MAZE DARKLY

The crocodile crawled onto the shore and chased the three. Eerey and her two companions hid in a crevice of glassy rock. The hiding place was not very deep. The crocodile put its long, thin snout into the narrow opening.

The croc snapped its enormous jaws, full of teeth as long as Edict's forearm, open and shut in an attempt to capture one of them. Eerey couldn't stifle her scream as they huddled against the back of the crevice. This caused Edict and then Guy to shout in fear at the crocodile. These noises did nothing to deter the enormous monster.

The jaws finally clamped on something solid. It pulled at Edict's tie and began to drag the boy out of the crevice. Eerey and Guy grabbed the back of Edict's jacket and tried to pull against the powerful creature. The crocodile was too strong. Edict slowly but surely began to leave the enclosure.

Edict fell and the crocodile began to drag him over the ground. It tried to make short work of Edict with a quick swipe of its sharp teeth.

"Edict!" Eerey shouted as the jaws closed to devour her cousin.

Suddenly, the crocodile arched in pain as Loofah leapt and landed on its back. The monster released a shrill hiss as Loofah bucked and landed on its back again.

"Run!" the orangutaur shouted as he leapt one more time, sending the crocodile off balance. Its legs collapsed for a moment and it fell to the ground as the three rushed past. The orangutaur leapt off the crocodile's back and quickly ran past the other three, despite their own speed in escaping.

Loofah's attack on the crocodile gave them enough time to make it to the waterfall. With no further consideration as to what might be behind them, all four rushed through the wall of water.

The noise of the falls thundered as the water pelted and drenched them. They stumbled over the rough stones on the bottom, and finally onto the other side.

On the other side of the waterfall, the first thing they saw was an image of the three of them. Guy remained invisible as ever, but the reflections of his companions returned to them from the enormous mirror. The direction opened up to their left and right into darkened corridors. The mirrored wall stood in the center of an enormous cone of black, volcanic glass. Light poured in from a round hole in the ceiling high above at the top of the enormous cone.

Loofah's eyes widened as he looked at the walls of dark glass. "What is this place?"

"I think we are inside an extinct volcano," Eerey offered.

"It is a volcano," Edict replied with a nod. "I just hope it's extinct."

The travelers could not contemplate this very long as they heard something large follow them through the waterfall. The four turned to see the giant crocodile moving through the cascade of water. They could make out its figure as it copied the color of the falling liquid. It changed so often that it looked like a big, crocodile-shaped water spray as it moved toward them.

"Let's get going!" Guy suggested, a bit too late. His three companions had already run into the darkness on their left. Guy quickly followed suit.

Eerey glanced back to see the crocodile come up to the shiny wall. His skin quickly turned into the reflective properties of the black mirror. The crocodile could see his form in the mirror, if only vaguely. It bristled for a moment and opened its jaws wide.

"He thinks his reflection is another crocodile!" Eerey said with glee. "He'll stay there for a moment."

Edict looked back and nodded. "Yeah, but it won't fool him for long," he said. "We have to keep going."

The group continued as their eyes adjusted to the dim light given off through the mouth of the volcano. They came to an area where three other corridors lead away from the one they had chosen. The construction of these corridors consisted of the glassy, black rock and had ceilings. Someone had definitely built these corridors. The sharp, clean corners could not have occurred naturally.

"It looks like a maze," Loofah said.

"Which way should we go?" Guy asked.

"If it's a maze," Eerey replied, "it doesn't matter which direction we go. As long as we keep our left hand always against the wall, we'll get through the maze."

Loofah rubbed his chin thoughtfully. "Why not our right hand?"

Edict sighed. "It doesn't matter which hand we use. As long as we keep one hand on a wall and follow it around all the corners, we'll eventually get to the end of the maze."

"What's at the end of the maze?" Loofah asked.

Just then, they heard the sound of the enormous crocodile coming behind them. "Right now, it doesn't much matter what's at the end," Eerey replied. "We've got to get away from what's at the beginning!"

The youths went into the corridor on their right. Guy clasped Eerey's hand and took the lead. He kept his right hand against one wall of the maze. Eerey grasped her cousin's hand. Edict, in turn, caught Loofah's hand. They walked into a darkened corridor.

"It's dark in here," Loofah stated the obvious.

"Really?" Edict questioned sarcastically. "I hadn't noticed."

Eerey peered into the blackness. "I can see somewhat. There's just a bit of light in here, but that's enough." She kept her hands on the wall and felt the corners turn. "I still don't like the dark."

"Me either," Guy admitted.

As they walked along, a circle of light flashed suddenly from the ceiling and bounced off the mirrored walls. Guy buzzed loudly for just the quick moment when the light flooded in. All four of them let out a slight yelp at the noise and the flash of light.

The circle closed as quickly as it had opened. On the walls next to them appeared two glowing pictures. The lichen on the walls replicated the four in a pair of photographs made from glowing lichen. Apparently, Guy was visible in complete darkness, along with his companions, and had not changed fast enough to avoid being photographed. Now that the lichen colony glowed from the wall, they were invisible again.

The picture looked weird, Eerey's white dress appeared black and Edict's black suit appeared white. All of the colors appeared in their opposite colors as well. Their features in the picture recreated a look of shock and surprise.

"How did that happen?" Guy asked.

"We probably stepped on some sort of trigger and opened a hole in the ceiling to the outside light," Edict replied. "The light reflected from the ceiling and walls and affected the light sensitive lichen on the mirrored walls. This type of lichen must not glow until exposed to light."

Eerey nodded. "Just like a camera. The colors are opposite because the picture is just like a photographic negative."

"Well," Loofah shrugged. "At least we have a little light from the lichen."

Edict began to run his hand over the picture. "We'll get more light if we open the camera aperture."

"Aperture?" Guy asked.

"It's the round hole that opens in a camera to expose the film," Edict explained. "Can I stand on your back, Loofah?"

"Absolutely not!" Loofah replied. "Just because I look like a horse doesn't mean I'm a trick pony. Besides, I think I can reach it myself." Loofah stood on his hind legs and stretched in the dim light toward the ceiling. With his long arms and horse legs, he could reach high into the air. He groped around the ceiling for a few moments, until he said, "Ah! Here it is!"

Loofah pulled at the device, and in a moment light flooded in through the small hole. His companions covered their eyes.

"It's pretty bright," Eerey said.

"That's all right," Edict said. "It's reflecting down the

corridor."

They looked down the hallway. Mirrors covered the ceiling and walls, reflecting light and exposing the lichen further down the corridor. The lichen collected the light reflected off the mirrors and began to glow.

"That will help for a ways," Eerey said. She placed her hands on the wall again. The others grasped hands and they continued.

"Where do you think the alligator is?" Loofah asked.

"It's a crocodile," Eerey corrected. "I don't think he could fit in this corridor."

"That's a good thing," Guy replied, "except we probably can't go back that way."

Edict nodded. "We shouldn't go back anyway. We've been there already."

After a few more turns, they found themselves in another corridor of mirrors without a ceiling. The light from the volcano's mouth reflected off the mirrors. The travelers let go of each other's hands and the mirrors reflected everyone but Guy.

"There's no ceiling here," Edict said.

Loofah nodded. "I noticed that. I think everyone did."

"That's not all," Eerey pointed at the center of the passage. Two pieces of smooth black glass stood directly opposite of each other.

"Let's go check it out!" Loofah said.

The quartet walked toward the pieces of black glass in the center of the mirrored corridor.

Eerey looked at the piece of glass on the left side of the corridor and exclaimed, "It's Mister Cryptic!" On the other side of the clear piece of dark glass stood a figure of a tall man inside a small area, dressed in a black suit identical to Pen's except for the color. Gray hair fell in long strands over the shoulders of his tall, thin figure. His eyes stared straight forward, not seeming to see the Tocsins or the orangutaur. Of course, he couldn't see Guy.

"If that's Mister Cryptic," Guy said, "who's that guy?"

They turned around to look into the piece of dark glass on the right. It seemed an exact reflection of the figure across from it.

They looked back and forth between the two figures for a moment. Finally, the two images spoke in perfect unison to the party. Their voices sounded hollow as they droned bad poetry to the party:

> "Two Mister Cryptics, but only one to believe,
> For one speaks the truth, one always deceives.
> You can ask just one question by which to reveal,
> Which one is false, and which one is real.
> You should choose wisely to rescue your friend,
> Or you and the zoo will come to an end."

Loofah pulled at his chin hairs. "I wonder which one it is."

"Don't ask any questions!" Eerey said. "We only have one, and we'll have to use it well."

"I don't think we need to ask anything!" Edict said excitedly.

Eerey eyed him suspiciously. "Perhaps I should ask something." She moved toward the Mr. Cryptic on the left.

Edict moved to block Eerey. "Don't bother asking a question! he demanded."

"Edict!" Eerey protested. "What are you talking about? We have to ask a question!"

Edict smiled and shook his head. "No. I believe they will both lie to us, no matter what we ask."

Mister Cryptic

CHAPTER XIII
MISTER CRYPTIC

Eerey looked at Edict with skepticism. "How can you be certain they would both lie?"

Edict nodded his head. "I can be certain, and I am certain. Either one we ask a question will lie to answer. Neither of them are the real Mister Cryptic."

"How do you know?" Loofah broke in.

"I know," Edict replied, "because if one of them always lied, then the poem they recited together must be a lie, or else he couldn't have said it."

"I don't know," Loofah said. "They could have both been telling the truth."

"Not if one of them always lies," Edict reminded. "If you don't trust my judgment, maybe you can trust my cousin. She knows I'm right." He stared at Eerey.

Eerey nodded. "He's right-both of them had to be lying."

"Maybe they don't lie when they're reciting the poem," Guy pointed out.

"No," Eerey replied. "It says one *always* deceives."

With arms folded, Edict spoke emphatically; "There's no way around it. They are both lying."

Loofah shrugged. "Okay, then. We still have to make a choice."

Eerey stood between the Mr. Cryptics and said aloud, "We choose neither of you!"

"Look!" Guy said as he pointed at the figures. No one aside from Eerey could see where he pointed, but they all looked at the Mr. Cryptics. The figures inside began to melt into black puddles behind the glass. The puddles drained into holes at the bottom of the enclosures.

"Will I help you?" a voice asked, startling the quartet. They spun quickly to face Mr. Cryptic, now standing behind them. "You have helped me immensely."

"Mister Cryptic?" Edict asked.

Mr. Cryptic smiled. "You have no need to ask my identity. I may be unfamiliar with yours, however."

"Oh," Edict said nervously, "I'm Benedict Tocsin. The orangutaur is named Loofah, and we have an invisible friend with us named Guy Guess." Edict indicated Eerey last with a wave of his hand. "And this girl is purportedly my cousin, Eridona."

"Purportedly?" Eerey objected. "I am your cousin!"

"So you say," Edict replied. "I still haven't forgotten what you said about me in your letter."

Mister Cryptic pulled at the lapels of his jacket. "If you will furnish me with the details of the letter, perhaps we can clear this all up."

Eerey stepped forward. "Edict ruined my sunglasses, so I wrote you a letter asking for advice."

Mr. Cryptic held his hand out. "Give me your letter."

"She doesn't have it anymore," Edict said.

Mr. Cryptic looked at Eerey. "Please, describe its contents."

"Essentially," Eerey started, "I asked if you might give me advice on controlling a troglodyte."

"You wanted to control your cousin, not a troglodyte."

"Sometimes he acts like a troglodyte," Eerey protested.

"Yes," Mr. Cryptic nodded. "Sometimes troglodytes act like humans. That does not make them human. It's no insult to be called a troglodyte unless it is meant as an insult."

Eerey hung her head and sighed. Everyone remained silent for a long moment. Eventually, she lifted her head and turned to Edict. "I'm so sorry for calling you a troglodyte," she apologized.

Mr. Cryptic spoke to Edict and said, "You can tell me now how you came to be here at the Cryptoid Zoo."

"I came to deliver Eerey's message," Edict replied. "I spent the money for postage, so I delivered it by hand."

"You had promised your cousin it would be delivered?"

"Yes," Edict replied. His facial expression twisted. "I couldn't remember that before, you know." Mr. Cryptic kindly gestured for Edict to continue. "I've been hypnotized by the false Cryptic to forget!"

Mr. Cryptic shook his head. "No, you forgot because you wanted to get back at your cousin for what she said in the letter."

"That's not true!" Edict denied. "I did forget!"

"Yes, you did forget, but the false Cryptic did not hypnotize you. He suggested he might do something like that and you took the idea and forgot yourself."

Edict rubbed his chin. "Is that why I'm remembering so easily?"

"Absolutely. You are just now beginning to forgive your cousin for her comments."

"I still can't remember forgetting on purpose," Edict replied. He turned to his cousin. "I'm sorry Eerey if I forgot on purpose, even if I don't remember."

"Well, when you are finished forgetting," Mr. Cryptic assured, "you will remember on purpose. Meanwhile, we have pressing matters to attend."

"Yes," Edict nodded in agreement. "First of all, I don't want to be considered a troglodyte and be put back into your zoo."

Mr. Cryptic smiled. "Well, that will not be a problem if we stop Pendragon. Pendragon is a doppelganger. He kidnapped me and took my shape. He has fooled the workers and animals here."

Loofah waved his arms. "We know all that! When you're the curator again, I don't want to be caged up, either!"

"Ah," Mr. Cryptic replied, "there will not be caged animals in the Cryptoid Zoo when I return to running it. The cages came from the zoo I purchased years ago to start the Cryptoid Zoo. I have never caged the animals. Pen decided to use them again."

"You don't cage your animals?" Edict asked. "How do you keep them from eating each other and the guests?"

"We have no real guests," Mr. Cryptic informed. "The

Cryptoid Zoo is really for the tenants, though occasionally someone will come to visit. It is a friendlier atmosphere among the animals. Much like a cat and a dog can peacefully co-exist, the animals do not fight."

"What if they do?" Loofah asked.

"They do not," Mr. Cryptic said emphatically. "Or at least, they did not until Pendragon took over. Pen has hypnotized them into acting unruly."

"Our main concern right now," Edict broke in, "is to beat Pen and escape the Cryptoid Zoo."

Mr. Cryptic shook his head. "There will be no need of escape if we remove Pendragon. You will be able to leave freely. You will have great difficulties in leaving if we do not first deal with Pendragon directly. We must escape this maze."

"That might take a while," Eerey pointed out. "We can't go back the way we came, because we left a giant invisible crocodile there. We don't know how long the maze is."

"I know the way out," Mr. Cryptic offered. "If you'll follow me," he turned and waved his hand. "it won't take us too long at all. It is actually easier to know where you are going if you can't go back. It only leaves one direction to travel."

The group of four became five as they followed Mr. Cryptic through the maze. Mr. Cryptic did not hold onto the wall as he walked swiftly down the corridors. Even Loofah, with his four hoofs, had difficulty keeping up with the zoo's former curator. Mr. Cryptic grabbed a handful of lichen off the wall and held it in his hand. When they re-entered a darkened passage, it lit the passageway with pale green light.

"Why didn't I think of that?" Edict asked.

"Yes," Loofah agreed. "It'd be about time you did something, instead of making us do all the work!"

"That's not funny," Edict replied.

"That's because you have no sense of humor," Loofah reminded.

Eerey put her finger over her lips. "Hush! Keep your voices down. We don't want anyone to hear us."

The pair became silent as they tried to keep up with Mr. Cryptic. The tall man turned left, then left again. He turned right without taking a moment of consideration as if he had traveled this maze a thousand times before. Finally, he turned a corner where light came into the corridor again.

"Here we are at last!" Mr. Cryptic exclaimed with a smile. They stood on the edge of a deep, dark canyon. Mr. Cryptic stared into the darkness below.

"Where are we at last?" Guy asked.

"At the stairway," Mr. Cryptic said. "Just over there." He pointed to the wall of black, volcanic glass on the other side of the impassable black fissure.

"I don't see a stairway," Edict said as he gazed across.

"You may have noticed by now," Mr. Cryptic replied, "that you don't always see everything in the Cryptoid Zoo by using your eyes alone."

"Exactly," Guy piped in. The invisible boy poked at Edict's shoulder to illustrate a point.

"I, for one," Loofah huffed, "am sick of not being able to see stuff. We already did a stairway we couldn't see because it was dark. I've never even seen Guy. Then, there was that giant crocodile. Now, we can't see this set of stairs because they're invisible!"

"We have at least four other senses," Eerey reminded. "Perhaps we need to use those for a change."

"Which sense should we use?" Guy asked.

"If the stairs are invisible," Eerey mused, "and they don't smell, that eliminates two senses. They don't make noise, and we probably shouldn't taste them. The only thing left is the sense of touch."

"The stairway is not invisible," Mr. Cryptic assured. "You just cannot see it from here. It is hidden in the rock wall over there."

"Why did you build it like that?" Edict asked.

"Oh, I didn't build it," Mr. Cryptic replied. "It was like that when I got here."

Loofah scratched his chin. "Who built it, then?"

Mr. Cryptic shrugged. "I suppose the Morlocks built it a long time ago, when they used this part of the caverns. They've lived here for ages."

"All this is well and good," Eerey said, "except we can't get across."

"Why not?" Mr. Cryptic asked.

"Because of this large ditch in the ground," Edict stated.

"It will not be that bad," Mr. Cryptic assured. "It is not as deep as it looks."

"Even so," Loofah said, "it still looks pretty deep."

"Does it now?" Mr. Cryptic said. "Why not test it?"

"I don't even want to go near the edge," the orangutaur assured. "I could take a chance of falling in."

"The danger is in your mind my friend," Mr. Cryptic said. "However, you needn't try if you are afraid."

"Afraid?" Loofah balked. "An orangutaur is afraid of nothing!"

"You could have fooled me," Edict said. "If you're not afraid, check it out!"

Loofah huffed and thrust his fur-covered chest out. "I'll show you who's afraid!" He walked to the very edge of the cliff. Egged on by pride, he stared downward. Then, he slipped forward and fell over the edge. He let out a terrified yell, but his foot struck something a few inches below the edge.

"Hey!" he exclaimed as he stepped out onto a solid surface. "It's like the air is frozen!"

Edict walked over to edge and looked. "The air's not frozen," he informed the orangutaur. "It's all volcanic glass!"

"The abyss is usually darker than it is deep," Mr. Cryptic offered.

Edict stepped onto the glass, followed by Guy and Eerey. Mr. Cryptic walked onto the surface last.

"It is like walking on air!" Guy exclaimed. "It looks like we're floating!"

"Since glass is actually a slow moving liquid," Eerey said,

"we are floating - in a way."

Loofah shivered. "I don't like the sound of that."

"Do not worry," Mr. Cryptic assured. "Glass flows so slowly, it would take many years before you noticed any movement."

"Since we're on a solid surface," the orangutaur said, "maybe we could stop and eat? I'm starving." At the thought, Loofah's stomach grumbled loudly.

"Did you bring any food with you?" Edict asked. "If you didn't bring a lunch, there's nothing to eat."

"Of course I didn't!" Loofah retorted.

"I brought some *Chasville Gnaws* in my backpack," Eerey offered.

"Well, break them out!" Edict said excitedly. Then, he added, "Please."

Eerey unzipped her backpack as the party sat down. Eerey let Eightball out of the pack as she retrieved five *Chasville Gnaw* candy bars and a couple of bottles of soda.

Mr. Cryptic picked up the spider. "What an interesting specimen," he mused. "Do you know what kind it is?"

Eerey shook her head at the question. "I just found it in my bedroom."

Mr. Cryptic smiled. "Most scientists will never see a live one of these. It is a megarchne: a large, prehistoric spider. I've never seen one with legs this long."

"You've seen one before?" Eerey asked.

"I have," Mr. Cryptic replied. "We have some in the zoo."

"I thought the megarchnes were extinct," Edict said as Eerey handed out the candy bars.

Mr. Cryptic nodded. "Many Cryptozoological animals are just creatures thought to be extinct."

"I wish they were!" Loofah shuddered. "It's creepy!"

"The Cryptoid Zoo is for creatures some people wish were extinct," Mr. Cryptic said. "It is sort of a wildlife refuge for all the animals that are not supposed to exist."

"It makes me nervous," Loofah said. "Could you put it away, Eerey?"

"It hasn't been out in hours," Eerey reminded. "It won't hurt you. You didn't like being caged up, either."

"I'm not a bug," Loofah reminded.

"Eightball's not a bug," Eerey replied. "He's a pet."

Loofah sighed and sat down. "I suppose you're right." The orangutaur began eating his candy bar, although he never took his eyes of Eightball for a moment.

The party finished their strange meal and prepared to continue. Eerey put Eightball into the backpack once more and asked, "Where do we go now, Mister Cryptic?"

"Shush!" Loofah whispered harshly. "What is that noise?"

Everyone listened. The screeching noise began very quietly, as if it were some distance away. It grew louder and closer.

"Bats!" Guy shouted. "There's not enough light down here for me to buzz, either!"

"Let's get out of here!" Loofah suggested as he began to run down the river of dark glass.

"Where are you going?" Edict shouted to Loofah, but the orangutaur ran on all four legs. The other four ran after him just as the bats appeared over the river of glass. The sound of their shrieks filled the air.

"There they are!" Edict shouted. "They're chasing us!"

"We need to get to the stairs," Eerey suggested.

"What about Loofah?" Guy asked.

"Loofah!" Edict shouted again, but it was too late. One of the fast-flying bats flew down and grabbed onto Eerey's backpack with its claws. Eerey's shrieks joined the cacophony of the giant bats as the bat carried her into the air.

"Eerey!" Edict shouted before being grabbed himself around his shoulders. Edict saw another grasp at something unseen and lift up again. The bat began to disappear. Presumably, it had caught Guy.

Edict struggled as he watched Loofah run. As fast as the orangutaur's horse legs moved, the bats flew faster. Soon, one caught the orangutaur's back and lifted him into the air. Edict hoped Mr. Cryptic had escaped, but his heart sank when he saw a bat carrying Mr. Cryptic by the waist. The bats had captured everyone.

The bats flew on, clutching the captives in their claws. The screeches continued as they used the sounds to navigate the vast volcano mouth. They headed toward the opening at the top of the volcano.

"Don't worry!" Guy shouted. "If they're headed outside, I'll start buzzing when the sunlight hits me! They'll have to drop us!"

"That's not so good," Loofah shouted, "if they have to drop us when we're a hundred feet in the air!"

"You're right!" Guy replied. "That's not so good!"

"Why would Pen risk losing us?" Edict asked.

"Perhaps Pen does not want us!" Mr. Cryptic replied. "Perhaps he *wants* the bats to drop us!"

Suddenly, the round mouth of the volcano seemed to be everyone's death-sentence. They all watched as the light grew brighter and larger. Guy began to buzz audibly.

"Knock it off, Guy!" Edict shouted.

"I can't help it!" Guy replied, trying to hold back tears. "I'm sorry!"

"It's not your fault!" Eerey said.

"No it's not," Guy said. "But there is something I can do to fix it! Goodbye, friends!"

Eerey, unlike the others, could see Guy's actions. The sunlight greatly impaired her vision, but she could see Guy had taken off his shoe. Holding the shoe between his teeth, he began to climb the bat that carried him. The bat struggled with its legs to control Guy, but the invisible boy grabbed onto the bat's coarse hair. With great effort, Guy pulled himself up. When he felt close enough, he held tightly onto the bat's hair with his right arm and took the shoe out of his mouth.

"Don't do it Guy!" Eerey cried out.

Guy buzzed so loudly now that the bats started to become erratic. Several of the bats flew into the walls of the volcano. Thankfully, they were not carrying anyone. "Here's something for you to eat!" he shouted at the bat, and shoved his shoe in the creature's mouth.

With the shoe stuffed in its mouth, the bat could not make noise to direct it. It could no longer use its radar. Frightened, it flew about uncontrolled. The last thing Eerey saw before the sunlight became too great for her was Guy's bat hitting the side of the volcano's mouth.

"Guy!" she shouted, but to no avail. The buzzing grew quieter, and finally became silent in the yawning maw of the volcano's mouth.

Torrance, the Minotaur

CHAPTER XIV
THE INVISIBLE PREDICAMENT

Tears welled-up in Eerey's eyes as the bats flew into the bright sunlight. Edict looked over at her and asked, "Are you crying, Eerey?"

"No," Eerey replied. "The sun hurts my eyes." She wasn't too certain if it was the sun or Guy. He had sacrificed himself to save the others and Eerey wouldn't forget him. Without the buzzing to bother them, the bats flew quite gracefully through the air. Though bats are usually nocturnal, they can fly as well in either the daytime or night.

"What happened to Guy?" Edict asked.

"His bat crashed," Eerey said. "He fell to his death!"

Indeed, Eerey's assertion that his bat crashed held true. She had seen it, so the second part of her statement seemed an obvious conclusion. No one could survive a fall from such a great height.

However, she did not see how the ever-resourceful Guy Guess grasped the wings of the unconscious bat and pulled them apart like a kite. She failed to see how he used the bat's giant wings to glide through the air.

It took Guy a moment to figure out how to steer the strange aircraft. He peered into the darkness for a place to land. He chose the long river of black glass as a natural runway. He aimed the bat in that direction by pulling at the wings. Although he was new to this task, he succeeded in clumsily controlling the flight. As he approached the river, he pulled on the wings to offer some wind resistance and slow his descent.

He steered the bat awkwardly to the smooth surface, trying to land as gently as possible. He bore the bat no ill will for its attack on him and hoped to save its life as well as his own. Guy rolled off the bat and slid for some distance next to it. Finally, both figures slowed to a halt.

Guy sat up and checked himself for injuries. He was a bit sore from the landing, but not seriously hurt. He stood and walked over to the bat. He heard breathing from the unconscious creature and sighed in relief. In his opinion, the bat would recover. 'Perhaps I should become a doctor,' he mused.

He walked over to the rock wall where Mr. Cryptic had indicated an opening existed. He ran his hands along the rocks, looking for a crack in the wall that might open a hidden door.

As he sought for the opening, a creature appeared from the wall farther down. It had the figure of a young man in a gray business suit, with the head and horns of a bull. Guy moved against the wall and tried not to make any noise, aside from the very slight buzzing that couldn't be helped.

The figure looked at the bat that lay on the river of volcanic glass. It looked around and sniffed the air. Finally it shouted, "I know you're in here! I saw the photo you left in the beginning of the maze. I'm Torrance. You can call me Tory, for as much good as it will do you. I'm a minotaur and the guardian of this labyrinth. You won't get past me to leave."

"You'll never find me," Guy replied.

Tory looked directly at where Guy's voice came from. "You're invisible, aren't you? It doesn't matter. You're not getting past me. Your friends may have escaped after releasing the fake Mister Cryptic, but you won't."

"The fake Mister Cryptic?" Guy quizzed. "Who told you that?"

"The real one told me he kept a dangerous imposter he'd captured in the case," Torrance replied, "and now you've let him escape!"

"The one who told you that was the fake," Guy replied.

Tory shook his head. "I don't believe you. Prove it to me."

"Of course, I can't," Guy admitted. "Not until we find the real Mister Cryptic again and ask him. We are trying to help him get rid of the doppelganger."

Tory ran his hand along his horn. "What if you're lying?"

Guy shrugged. "If I'm lying, you can find out," he suggested.

"I have to guard the labyrinth," Tory said. "It's my job, and I'm not going to let you through on something I don't know is true. You can't sneak past me, either. I can't see you, but I'll find you if you try to get by."

Guy knew Tory told the truth. He had no choice. He would have to escape the maze before he could escape the zoo. Guy sat down and began planning.

Pen
(evil doppelganger-looks like Mr. Cryptic but with rows
of sharp teeth)

CHAPTER XV
PEN REVEALS HIS PLAN

The bats continued for some distance, carrying Eerey and her friends with them. Soon, a large power plant came into view. A wall of black volcanic glass surrounded it, and the bats flew over the wall and toward a large open window.

Mr. Cryptic and his young friends had to lift both (all four, in Loofah's case) of their legs to avoid hitting the base of the window. Rows of enormous electrical generators stood in the center of a large concrete room. A river of molten lava flowed between the generators in a streambed of volcanic glass. Big metallic wheels spun slowly as the lava pulled at the attached paddles.

The bats roughly placed their burdens on the floor as a door opened in one of the walls. Out stepped Pen, the false Mr. Cryptic, along with a dozen gorillas. The gorillas surrounded the prisoners and immediately began binding them with jungle vines.

Pen smiled as he approached his captives. "Ah, Mister Cryptic!" he said jovially. "It is nice of you to visit our facility. I am pleased your friends could join us." He nodded toward one of the gorillas. "I must apologize if the servants are a bit rough. Their training is very limited." He snapped his fingers and the gorillas came over and stood behind him.

Mr. Cryptic's expression became serious. "Do not cause more trouble for yourself, Pen. Release us this instant!"

Pen laughed a cold, hollow laugh. "You have no ability to make demands! All of you are at my mercy now." His eyes narrowed into thin slits. "I needn't remind you I have very little mercy." He looked at the group. "I see your invisible friend is not with you. What happened?"

"His bat crashed," Edict said.

Eerey looked at Pen. "What will you do with us now?"

Pen pointed a finger at Eerey. "That's a very good question my dear. Why, I intend to watch the volcano destroy the entire zoo, and all of you along with it."

"Can he do that?" Edict asked Mr. Cryptic.

Mr. Cryptic nodded in reply. "This facility has utilized geothermal energy for years. The volcano is not active as long as the flow of lava continues through the plant. It is a way to keep the island safe and generate energy at the same time. If he stops the flow of lava, the volcano will back up and explode. The island will be devastated. I expect he's planned this for some time."

Pen smiled at them. "You say I planned it as if there's a possibility I may fail," he said. "It's all as easy as a flick of the switch," He turned to the wall and put his hand in the direction of a large lever with the words 'open' and 'closed' written beside it. It was in the 'open' position for the moment. "That switch, in particular. I will close the sluice, and the volcanic reactions will begin."

"Why would you destroy the zoo?" Eerey asked.

"I plan to use the DNA I've sampled to start a chain of exotic cuisine restaurants," Pen replied. "I will make money hand over fist. Unfortunately, there could be future competitors if the zoo remains."

"You're crazy!" Loofah chimed in. "You'll be killed too!"

"I will not," Pen informed. "The giant bats will fly me to the mainland with the samples I've collected."

"Oh," Loofah said. "I hadn't thought of that."

Pen smiled. "While you were thinking about bananas and blueberries, my orangutaur friend, I planned carefully over the last few months while the real Mister Cryptic remained... indisposed."

"You cannot destroy the animals," Mr. Cryptic growled. "I won't allow it."

Pen sneered. "You are in no position to disallow it Mister Cryptic," he reminded. He reached over and pulled the lever in front of his horrified captives. A loud, grinding noise filled the air. The handle landed in the 'closed' position, and the lava ceased its flow.

Pen removed an oddly shaped wrench from his pocket and carefully removed the handle from the wall. He put it in the pocket of his long, grayish purple jacket.

Mr. Cryptic gritted his teeth and snarled; "You will not get away with this, Pen. I swear it."

"Now now, Mister Cryptic, please," Pen teased. "There is no swearing allowed in my house. In twenty-four hours, there will be nobody on the entire island left to swear!"

Pen whistled, and a moment later giant bats flew through the windows. Their squealing noise reverberated off the walls of the power plant as Pen laughed out loud. One of the bats grasped his shoulders and lifted him into the air. "Enjoy your stay!" he shouted. "I regret it will be such a short one!" The bats flew out of the windows and over the horizon.

The gorillas lumbered out of the room in a haphazard procession. The group struggled against their bonds. Loofah, being the strongest, managed to grasp his ropes and tear them apart. He rushed over to release the others.

"We must open the sluice again!" Edict shouted as Loofah untied him.

Mr. Cryptic shook his head. "That lever is specifically designed. We cannot open the sluice without it."

"Then, the island is doomed?" Eerey asked.

"Not if we can get to the sluice for the main flow," Mr. Cryptic replied. "If we open that sluice it will relieve the pressure and the danger will be eliminated, but it is on the other side of the island. It may take some time to get to it, but we have 24 hours. One thing Pen forgot about the giant bats, is they only respond to commands while on the island."

(At nearly the same time Mr. Cryptic said this, Pen discovered the truth of the statement and soon found himself swimming ashore after the bats dropped him into the ocean. He could have turned into a bat and flown, but he'd never learned how to fly.)

    After Loofah had removed all their bonds, the party started on their journey across the island to stop its destruction.

Bigfoot

CHAPTER XVI

INTO THE WOODS

Darkness still covered the island as they left the power plant. The moon helped light their surroundings as they stood there deciding on a course of action to take.

"Which direction?" Edict asked.

"The lava to produce the energy flows from the East," Mr. Cryptic replied. He used his index finger to point out the direction. A thick carpet of tall trees covered the area. "We must travel through the forest. A journey, they say, begins with the first step. There will be many steps before this journey is completed." He started walking toward the East. They all followed him into the thick forest. The canopy of branches and leaves blotted out the moonlight.

As they walked along, an idea came to Eerey. "What about the giant bird, Atlanta?" she suggested. "She could fly us across the island!"

"That is a good idea Eerey," Mr. Cryptic agreed. "Unfortunately, Atlanta is just about where we need to be ourselves. It would take as long to get to Atlanta as to get to the sluice."

"We don't all need to go," Loofah reminded. "I could carry Mister Cryptic there."

Mr. Cryptic shook his head. "Again, that's another good idea, but you would wear yourself out after a few miles. You are not a pack mule, Loofah." Loofah blushed. "Besides, the sluice for the main flow is complicated, and takes five people to run it. All of us must go, and we must all go together."

"But we don't have five right now," Eerey reminded. "Not without Guy."

Mr. Cryptic shrugged. "We need another party member. If

we do not find someone, the island is doomed and us along with it."

"I'm sure we can find someone else," Edict said.

"I certainly hope so," Eerey added.

"Is there anybody in the forest?" Loofah asked.

"I grew up in this forest," Mr. Cryptic replied. "I have some relatives here."

"You grew up in a forest?" Eerey asked. "Were you raised by wolves or something?"

Mr. Cryptic chuckled. "Oh, no! Nothing so exotic!"

"That reminds me," Edict said. "I thought we'd see a Bigfoot, but we haven't yet. I wanted to see one while we're here."

"Are you certain?" Mr. Cryptic asked. Before Edict could reply, a large, hairy creature leapt onto the path in front of them with a growl. Its thick, brown hair and large feet helped Edict identify the creature, but its teeth clinched it for him. "Bigfoot!" Edict exclaimed.

"Watch out!" Loofah warned as the creature rushed at them. It grasped Mr. Cryptic with its pair of elongated arms and began to crush him.

Eerey rushed at the creature and beat on its arms with her clenched fists. "Let go of him!"

Mr. Cryptic just laughed. "Stop, Eerey! All is not as it appears!"

The Bigfoot creature laughed as well. He released Mr. Cryptic and spoke; "It's nice to see you've made yourself some friends, Justin! I've been following you since you entered the forest, and saw the conversation led to an opportunity to introduce myself. And it is so good to see you again! You haven't been around for a while! I wondered when you would make time for your father!"

"Father?" Edict queried.

"I have been indisposed," Mr. Cryptic said to the creature. "I am sorry, Father." He turned to Edict and Eerey and explained; "As I said before, I was not raised by wolves. What an absurd idea!" Mr. Cryptic chuckled at the thought. "Bernard found me in the woods as a child and raised me as his own. As you know by now, my first name is Justin, and I am a Bigfoot by upbringing."

"This is excellent!" Edict said. He walked over to Bernard and held his hand out. "I've always wanted to shake hands with a Bigfoot! If I may, Bernard…"

Bernard accepted Edict's hand. "Technically, I'm a Sasquatch. It's preferable to being named after your shoe-size. Once we know each other better, maybe you'll call me friend."

"I'd like that," Edict replied with a grimace. Bernard held his hand too hard, but Edict didn't object. "I hope I didn't offend you." At the end of a hearty shake, Edict retrieved his hand and put it in his coat pocket.

Bernard held his hand up to Edict and smiled. "No need to apologize." He then turned to Mr. Cryptic. "So, what brings you here?"

"We are on a mission to stop the destruction of the island," Mr. Cryptic replied. "A doppelganger has taken my identity and set the volcano on an explosive path."

"Can you get there in time?" Bernard asked.

Mr. Cryptic shrugged. "I hope so."

"You can help us," Eerey interjected. "We need another set of hands."

Bernard shook his head. "It can't be done," Justin agreed. "As the King of the Forest, Bernard will have to remain to protect the woodland creatures if we fail to stop the volcano."

Bernard nodded. "I wish you all the speed and skill you'll need, but I can't help you. I'm sworn to guard the forest." He pointed to a path through the woods. "If you follow that trail, you can get to the lava sluice faster. I'll put out word to the creatures to not bother you."

Morlocks

CHAPTER XVII
EDICT, THE GOLDEN 'LOCK

The party progressed along the path Bernard had pointed out to them. Despite the scratching tree branches and the uneven ground, the party made good time. In a few hours, they came again to the non-existent door that Loofah opened earlier. They could see the zoo's cages in the distance. They all leaned against the wall.

"Can't we stop and sleep?" Loofah complained. "I'll be no good if we don't."

"We likely don't have time," Eerey informed with a yawn, "but I suppose we could sit down and rest for a moment." They all sat on the ground against the wall. Despite their best attempts to stay awake, they all fell into a deep sleep. None of the night sounds woke them, including the beginning of the volcano's low grumbling. The light of dawn woke them inside thin haze of volcanic smoke.

"We've been asleep!" Eerey exclaimed. "The volcano's become active!"

"We're too late!" Loofah wailed.

Mr. Cryptic shook his head. "The volcano is simply letting off a little steam. We should still have time, though I'm concerned for those living in the volcano."

"Do you mean the Morlocks?" Edict asked. "Are they in danger?"

"If the lava fills the caverns," Mr. Cryptic said with a shrug, "hopefully they can get out."

Edict's eyes widened. "But Pen hid the way out! We've got to help them!"

"As much as it pains me," Eerey replied. "We have to stop the volcano. The Morlocks can't be helped right now."

"Then let me help them," Edict insisted.

"We don't have enough of us to spare," Eerey said. "With

Guy gone, we're one short already."

"You'll have to find two more then," Edict demanded. "Can't you see, Eerey? It's my destiny. I am the Morlocks' Golden 'Lock, and I can help them escape the destruction!"

"How will you find your way out?" Loofah asked.

"Do you still have the rope you made from your hair?" Loofah nodded a reply to Edict's question. "Give it to me."

Loofah did as requested. Edict took the rope and slung it over his shoulder. "I'll use this to find my way back."

Mr. Cryptic put his hand on Edict's shoulder and smiled. "If you are serious, we will not stop you. Go, and we will return if we succeed."

Edict turned to Loofah. "I'll need the key."

"I can't give you a key," Loofah replied. "I only had the key when I thought the door was real."

"Think it's real again," Edict begged. "Please, the Morlocks' lives depend on your faith."

Loofah furrowed his brow for a moment. He looked at the door, then at Edict. Finally he said, "I'll try, but I'm not promising anything."

Loofah stared hard at the door. He concentrated on believing the door was real. He repeated to himself, "The door is there," over and over again. After long moments, he turned to Edict. "Let me have your jacket."

Edict removed his jacket, and Loofah rummaged through the pockets until he pulled out a key. "See?" Loofah said. "You had the key all along!" This amazed everyone but Loofah as he put the key in the lock and turned it. The door disappeared as it had previously done. Loofah placed the key back in Edict's pocket and returned the jacket.

Edict smiled. "Thank you, friend!" he said. After saying his goodbyes and shaking everyone's hand, he walked through the door.

The stairwell became dark as the door that wasn't there returned. Edict cursed his planning for not having thought to bring a flashlight or candle. Some Golden 'Lock he was; not being very prepared to fulfill his duties as rescuer. Thankfully, he remembered how many steps Eerey counted the first time they'd taken the journey, and he began counting the long journey into the darkness.

As he neared the last few steps, he tied the rope to a secure rock that jutted from the ground and began to unravel it. He knew it wouldn't last for the entire length of the stairwell, but he could use it as a short guide to find the stairs again.

The last step was exactly the 1576th stair. He still had some rope left, having tied the rope off at the 1550th stair. A reddish glow allowed him to see in the cavern as lava flowed into the far section. The red-hot, glowing rock moved quickly through the cavern. He saw the Morlocks standing on a tall boulder, surrounded by the moving lava. He hadn't noticed them at first as his eyes adjusted to the crimson light.

"Come this way!" he shouted to them. "This is the way out!"

"It's the Golden 'Lock!" one of the female Morlocks shouted.

"No," a male replied with a frown. "He lies! There is no longer a way out. He's not a true prophet. He's not even a Morlock. We're all doomed!"

"It doesn't matter if I'm the Golden 'Lock or not!" Edict protested. "I know the way out!"

A Morlock carrying a staff came to the edge of the rock. It was Asentzio, the leader he'd met before. "If you are here to save us," he said, "prove to us that you believe in us before you ask us to believe in you. Come to us on the rock. Then, we will believe you have our interests at heart."

Edict looked at the lava around the rock. He gauged the distance and gulped. He had never leapt that far before. It seemed impossible, but he was willing to try. As he walked to the edge of the lava, he felt the heat singe the hair on his body. He closed his eyes, breathed deeply from the air full of toxic volcanic fumes, and took a leap of faith across the deadly chasm. He felt his feet land on the warm rocks where the Morlocks stood. He nearly fell backwards, and opened his eyes to see the lava behind him. Something grasped his arm and pulled him upright onto the safety of the boulder.

Asentzio smiled as he pulled Edict away from the lava with the crook of his staff. "I, for one, believe you Edict. Only great concern could cause one to take such a dangerous action. Lead us away from here."

"Follow me," Edict ordered. He turned, and repeated the amazing leap. He noticed the heat from the lava had singed away all the fur on his face and hands, though his suit remained intact. The Morlocks with their powerful legs leapt from the rock to safety on the other side of the lava.

Edict searched for the rope he had left out, but he could not see it. Instead, a stream of lava suddenly erupted and blocked the path in the direction of the stairs. He could see the stairs clearly in the crimson glow, but the new stream of lava proved too large to jump. The rope had apparently burned, as Edict saw a line of ashes leading up the stairs.

"What do we do now?" one of the Morlock children asked.

"Now," Asentzio said, "we wait on the Golden 'Lock to perform a miracle."

"Performing miracles is not something I know how to do," Edict replied. "I do think a trick is in order, however." Edict closed his eyes once more and walked into the stream of lava. The Morlocks gasped as they watched him turn into a pillar of flame and melt into the lava.

"The Golden 'Lock!" a girl shouted. "He walked right into the lava, and it incinerated him!"

The girl could not have been more right or more wrong in the same sentence. While it was true he had walked right into the lava, it was not true that it had incinerated him.

Being familiar by now with Pen's hypnotic traps set on the stairwell, Edict made careful observation of the lava stream. The gravity should have made the lava settle at the lowest point of the cavern floor. Instead, it seemed to choose the slightly higher area right in front of the wall.

If the lava stream defied gravity, Edict reasoned, it must be an illusion. He hoped he was right as he stepped forward. As any good illusion is designed to do, it compensated for Edict's presence and made it look to the Morlocks as if he'd been destroyed in the fire. Instead, he made it comfortably and safely to the stairs.

Edict attempted to call back to the Morlocks, but their hypnotized state wouldn't allow them to see or hear him. He walked back over the floor and stood next to Asentzio. "The lava's not there, Asentzio," Edict said. Still under the hypnotism, Asentzio did not hear him the first time. Edict shouted at him. "The lava is not real!"

Asentzio's eyes widened and he looked about. Seeing only the Morlocks, he exclaimed, "I hear the voice of the Golden 'Lock! It whispers to me and says; 'the lava is not real'."

Edict smiled and shouted again. "The lava is not there! Walk through it, the way I did!"

"The whisper is unmistakable!" Asentzio said excitedly. He took a deep breath and walked forward. As with Edict, it appeared the flames and heat consumed Asentzio. However, Asentzio felt no discomfort and discovered the stairs. Edict had followed him and stood beside the Morlock leader. Edict's grin displayed his pleasure.

Asentzio bowed to Edict. "You showed me the way!"

Edict shook his head. "You showed yourself the way. Now, we have to show the others the way."

Edict and Asentzio crossed over to the Morlocks and shouted loudly until all the Morlocks heard them in a whisper.

"It's Asentzio and the Golden 'Lock!" one woman exclaimed.

"I hear it too!" a man said.

"They are telling us to cross the lava!" a young girl agreed.

"I, for one, refuse to cross the lava," one of the men said. "I've seen two people destroyed by it, and I don't wish to be destroyed!" A handful agreed with him and stayed behind as they watched all the others walk into the lava and the heat burn them to cinders. They wailed and tried to stop the others, but one-by-one, those who wished walked into the lava.

When all but the few who remained had crossed successfully,

Edict looked back at the stragglers. "We've got to save them!" he said to Asentzio.

"How can we get them across if they won't listen to us?" Asentzio asked.

Edict held up his rope made from orangutaur hair. "There's always the physical way."

In a few moments, a rope appeared around the waists of the remaining Morlocks. They soon found themselves dragged, one by one, into the lava. They protested and cried while their companions attempted to pull them back, but with the larger group of Morlocks pulling against them, they could not stop the rope. As soon as they got to the other side and Edict explained that the lava was an illusion, they helped pull their friends across. In no time, all the Morlocks gathered on the stairs.

"Is everyone here?" Edict asked. Asentzio nodded. Edict went on, "The volcano's dangerously close to exploding. I think you will remember this staircase from before." The Morlocks nodded or said they remembered. "Good. We need to get out of here as quickly as possible."

Edict began ascending the long flight of stairs with Asentzio and the Morlocks close behind. Edict thought the darkness and gloom seemed deeper on the return trip than it had in the descent. The reddish glow of the lava beneath reflected around the cavern. It even seemed to be getting brighter.

Edict turned to look back down the stairs, and saw the lava rising behind them. "Hurry!" he urged. "The lava is coming!"

The Morlocks looked behind them and began to panic. "Don't panic!" Asentzio shouted too late. The Morlocks began pushing and shoving at each other. In their haste, they could barely move as they tried to push forward.

"What can we do?" Asentzio asked. He had managed to avoid the rush, and he and Edict stood looking at the mass of Morlocks and the lava rising behind them.

Edict considered for a moment as the lava continued to rise. "Do the Morlocks know how to play leap frog?"

"What's that?"

"It's a child's game where one child leaps over the other's back. If they act in an orderly manner, the Morlocks will move quickly. With their powerful legs, they should cover the stairs in no time at all."

"I think I understand," Asentzio said. He explained the game to the Morlocks, and soon they had set up four lines across. Each Morlock would leap over the one in front, and they in turn would leap. The sight proved something to behold as the Morlocks leapt up the staircase. Edict and Asentzio ran after them, with the fast moving lava at his heels.

After several dozen steps, the lava slowed. "I think we're past the dangerous point now," Edict yelled to the Morlocks. "The lava's still coming, but once we're out of the staircase we should be fine." The Morlocks continued the game, even though they had heard him.

"They shouldn't wear themselves out," Edict said.

"The Morlocks have a lot of stamina," Asentzio replied.

When Edict and Asentzio arrived at the door, they found the Morlocks making useless attempts to open it. The reddish glow from the lava far below barely lit the area.

"Step aside please," Edict said. "I have the key." He reached in his pocket, and was surprised he felt the key Loofah had given him earlier-the orangutaur's imaginary key! The Morlocks cleared the way, and Edict stepped up to the door.

Edict searched the doors surface with his fingers. He couldn't find a keyhole or a door handle on the door's inside. Although he knew the door wasn't there, he doubted he could use the same trick as he'd used on the lava illusion. He looked back, and saw the slowly moving lava creep toward them. The lava cast off a red glow, illuminating the area.

Edict had another idea. He turned to Asentzio. "Here's the key to the door," he told the Morlock leader as he retrieved the key from his pocket. "There's a keyhole on the door, but I don't see as well as you do in dim light. Perhaps you can find it when I can't." Edict knew that the door existed only in the minds of the Morlocks and himself. If Asentzio believed Edict, he would find a keyhole that wasn't there before.

Asentzio took the key and began running his fingers over the door's surface. He searched it more than once before he turned again to Edict. "I can't find it," he sullenly admitted.

Edict looked at the Morlock leader. "Please, try one more time."

Asentzio sighed and started running his hands over the door again. He went over the door several more times, to no avail. Finally, he sat down. "It's not there!" he said. "I'm sorry."

Edict furrowed his brow. He looked at the rising lava behind them. It would reach the Morlocks when it rose a few dozen steps. "It must be somewhere," he said as he examined the door.

Asentzio beat the stair he sat on with his palms. "I tell you, it's not there!" he shouted in frustration. "Take this accursed key back!"

Edict stared at Asentzio's hand. The key did not hold as much interest for him the red mark in the center of the palm. "What's that?"

Asentzio looked at his hand. His eyes widened. "It's from when I hit the floor!" The shape of the red mark looked like a large keyhole. Asentzio went back to the stair and felt around. Sure enough, he found a keyhole in the top of the stair. He put the key inside, and the door began to disintegrate.

The Morlocks cheered as they walked into the bright sun. They covered their eyes from the blinding rays.

Asentzio stood before the Morlocks. He raised his staff above his head and spoke. "We are rescued, thanks to the Golden 'Lock!" A cheer arose in reply to the statement.

"I'm still not a Morlock," Edict whispered to Asentzio.

"That's not how we'll tell the story," Asentzio replied in a low voice. "Today, you have earned the right to be called a Morlock."

Edict frowned for a moment, then slowly smiled. "I'll bear the name proudly," he replied. "I've decided there's nothing wrong with being a troglodyte, and it's good to be a Morlock. Even though I'm human, there's a bit of the other two in me."

Tyrannosaurus Rex (Pen's transformation)

CHAPTER XVIII
AN INVISIBLE BOY SIGHTING

The island rumbled with volcanic activity and the ground occasionally shook slightly. The grumbles grew louder and became constant the more they traveled. They walked past many of the zoo's cages on their journey, but they were all empty. There wasn't an animal to be seen anywhere.

"Who let out the animals?" Loofah asked.

Mr. Cryptic shrugged. "I am sure I do not know," he replied. "Perhaps it was Jack. We can worry about that problem later. Our first priority is to stop the volcano."

"We need two more people to do that," Loofah reminded. "It's too bad we didn't take Bernard along."

No one said anything, but everyone wished Guy and Edict were there. Eerey let out a sigh. She hoped Edict succeeded in his mission, and she missed Guy.

As she thought about this, the three travelers heard a voice shout, "Eerey! Loofah! Mister Cryptic!" The constant rumbling of the volcano nearly drowned out the words, and the sound of Guy's buzzing.

They all turned around. "It's Guy!" Eerey shouted. She ran over to the invisible boy and threw her arms around his neck. "We all missed you!"

"Not so tight," Guy complained. He squirmed to escape Eerey's grip.

"I don't see him," Loofah said as he peered where Eerey stood.

"Did you ever see him?" Mr. Cryptic replied.

Loofah shrugged. "Not that I remember."

"What are you doing here?" Guy asked as he and Eerey rejoined the other two.

"We're going to the other volcanic sluice," Loofah informed.

"We've got to open it and stop the volcano."

Mr. Cryptic nodded. "It is a good thing you came along when you did, Guy. We needed more hands to operate the sluice."

"I'm going to do the best I can," Guy said.

"We will all have to do our best to stop this volcano," Eerey put in. "We don't have any choice. If we fail, we'll be destroyed with the island."

They came to a particularly large, empty cage. A building exactly like the power station where Pen had shut off the volcanic flow stood behind it. They all stopped to look at the building.

"Here is the moment of truth," Mr. Cryptic said. They continued walking toward the building. In a few moments, they stood in front of the doors painted as grey as a dark cloud.

"How do we get in?" Eerey asked.

"Through the door," Guy replied. "I'm assuming they don't lock it."

"Why would you assume that?" Loofah queried.

Guy shrugged. "Why should they lock it?" With that, he turned the handle. The door swung open invitingly. "See?"

Loofah whistled as they entered an enormous room with large power generators. "Whew! Those are some big generators!"

"Indeed," Mr. Cryptic agreed. "They power the entire island completely with energy taken from the volcano and the island's unique magnetic properties." A river of lava flowed through the center of the room, confirming Mr. Cryptic's statement. A bridge crossed over the lava to the other side.

"The island is magnetic?" Eerey asked.

Mr. Cryptic nodded. "Yes. That is why metal airplanes cannot fly here."

"If airplanes can't fly here," Loofah pondered aloud, "and cars can't drive here because it's an island, how did we get here in a truck?"

"A cargo plane brought you here," Mr. Cryptic explained. "It flew high enough above the island that it wasn't affected by the magnetism and dropped the truck."

Eerey's eyes widened. "Is Atlanta strong enough to carry a

truck?"

Mr. Cryptic shook his head. "No. Parachutes carry the truck to the ground."

"I don't remember that!" Loofah protested.

"You would not remember," Mr. Cryptic said. "A sleeping gas fills the rear compartment before the truck is loaded onto the aircraft. It alleviates anxiety in the passengers. Most animals do not like flying, and fewer still enjoy a parachute ride."

Eerey began walking toward the bridge. "You can explain later. Right now, we must stop the lava flow."

"We still need one more to flip the switch," Loofah reminded as he walked to the edge of the bridge. "Shouldn't we find another first? I don't want to cross a river of boiling rock and have it be a wasted trip."

Suddenly, Edict burst through the door. He saw the three figures standing on the bridge, and Loofah on its edge. "Stop!" he shouted. "That's not Guy!"

The four figures looked at Edict in surprise. "Who are you?" Eerey asked.

Edict looked at his hands and remembered his encounter with the lava's heat burned the hair off his exposed skin. The ashes from his hair turned his skin gray. Eerey had never seen his features without hair before. "It's me, Edict! Lava burned off my hair, but don't you recognize my suit and voice?"

"That's not good enough," Loofah snarled. "You could still be Pen! He can look like anyone!"

"Yes!" Edict agreed. "And right now, he looks like Guy!"

"How would you know?" Eerey asked. "You can't see him."

Edict attempted to make eye contact with each one of them as he spoke. "I know because I just saw Guy and he's on his way here."

Loofah's eyes narrowed with distrust. "You couldn't have seen guy. He's invisible!"

Edict rolled his eyes. "A figure of speech, Loofah. I talked to him on my way here."

"If you tell us what Guy told you," Mr. Cryptic said, "we

can decide if you are telling the truth."

Eerey nodded. "Yes. Tell us where you saw Guy. Why didn't he come with you?"

"He's on the other side of the black wall. He heard me run by, and he called out. He said a minotaur showed him the way out of the volcano, but on the wrong side of the black wall. When I left, he said he'd try to find a way around the wall."

"How do you know it was him?" Loofah asked.

"I recognized his voice," Edict said.

Loofah continued the interrigation; "How did you know there was a fake Guy with us?"

"Because I heard him talking as I ran to catch you. My ears are keener than most people's. I tried to shout, but the volcano's too loud." Edict looked directly at Eerey. "Eerey, look into my eyes. You'll see it's really me, your cousin. I know I've been inconsiderate, but I've never meant to hurt your feelings. I can't help that I'm thick sometimes, as much as I'd like to. This is very important, Eerey. Look at Guy. Does he look different in any way?"

Eerey turned her head to observe the invisible boy's appearance. She looked at his facial features and clothes. She bristled slightly. Her eyes peered deeply at the figure. "Guy," she said, "who is that on your shirt?"

Guy offered a friendly, close-mouthed smile. "It's Cedrick Hardwicke, of course. He played the first Invisible Man in the movies. He's my hero."

Eerey shook her head. "You're wrong. Claude Rains played the Invisible Man in the first movie. You <u>are</u> Pen!"

Guy's expression fell. His eyes glowered as he displayed a row of sharp teeth. "So, you've figured it out, have you? It won't do you any good."

Guy's - or rather Pen's - face distorted as it began to grow and change. His mouth became elongated and his sharp teeth grew as he became visible. His nose became smaller and disappeared into the end of a growing snout. His skin became rougher and a pair of bony ridges started running along his back.

Pen had transformed into a giant crocodile like the one they'd faced underground. For a moment, all could see the *Gigantus Crocidilous Terribilous*. In the next moment, it took on the color of its surroundings with its camouflage properties and disappeared.

"We need to get off the bridge!" Eerey shouted too late. An enormous unseen crocodilian tail lashed out at Eerey and Mr. Cryptic. The enormous tail struck them both and flung them over the railing. Eerey screamed as she began to fall toward the lava. She reached out and caught the railing. Her feet dangled as the river of molten rock flowed beneath her. She looked to her left to see Mr. Cryptic likewise dangling from the railing.

"Mister Cryptic!" Loofah shouted as he rushed onto the bridge. Edict, not as close as Loofah, ran to the bridge as well. "Eerey!" he shouted.

"Stay back, Loofah!" Mr. Cryptic warned. Loofah continued, heedless of the danger. The invisible tail swung again and struck Loofah across his cheek. The powerful blow knocked the orangutaur unconscious and flung him off the bridge and back onto the floor.

Eerey struggled to lift herself up, but the invisible tail lashed out and violently struck the railing. The entire bridge rocked under the blow, causing Eerey and Mr. Cryptic to hang on for dear life.

Edict stopped on the other side of the bridge. He couldn't risk the giant crocodile killing him before he helped his cousin. He looked around for anything that might help him. His eyes rested on a catwalk above the bridge. "Hang on!" he shouted. "I'll be up on the catwalk!" He ran over to the steps for the catwalk and began to climb.

Meanwhile, Pen began to change shapes again. The crocodile appeared as a gray-skinned giant during the transformation. The skin turned from gray to blue as it began to grow even larger. In a very short time, the giant crocodile turned into a large tyrannosaurus rex.

"I will destroy you!" Pen, the dinosaur, roared in a voice

that rumbled with the now constant volcanic quakes.

Edict reached the catwalk and ran until he was right above the bridge. He pulled out Loofah's homemade rope and tied it to the railing. He tied the other end of the rope to himself and shouted, "I'm coming Eerey!" He held onto the rope and began to let himself down to the bridge.

Pen saw the dangling figure and leaned his jaws far over the lava stream. Edict tried to reel himself in again, but the powerful tyrannosaurus jaws clamped onto the rope and ripped it in half. The dinosaur's teeth lodged the rope between them like a piece of dental floss. Edict hung on as the tyrannosaur thrashed its head about trying to dislodge the unwelcome guest. The dinosaur's short arms flailed ineffectually at Edict, but the rope held.

The disruption gave Eerey and Mr. Cryptic a chance to climb to safety. Eerey rushed across the bridge to help Edict in his plight. Mr. Cryptic reached out to grab her. "Stop!" he shouted. "I will deal with this!"

Mr. Cryptic's long fingers managed only to catch the zipper on her backpack and pull it open. Eightball instantly escaped his unwelcome confines. He fell to the floor and ran in the direction of the dinosaur.

"Eightball!" Eerey yelled as she ran after the spider. "Come back!"

Mr. Cryptic ran after Eerey, but he could not catch up with her before she reached the tyrannosaurus and Edict. Eightball reached the dinosaur first, and not wanting to return to the backpack, began climbing the behemothian lizard. "Let go of my cousin!" Eerey demanded as she battered her fists against the dinosaur's foot, heedless of her own safety.

Everything went instantly haywire. Pen saw the large spider crawling up his leg and went into hysterics. He twirled around in a manner that might seem humorous if the circumstances were different. He knocked a tall vat of water into the lava with his tail, instantly creating a great deal of steam. With a mighty swing, he flung Edict free. Edict flew violently toward the molten river's far bank.

"Edict!" Eerey shouted. She couldn't see through the steam to discover what happened to him. She continued to beat on the tyrannasaurus' foot out of helpless anger. "If you hurt Edict, Pen, you're going to pay!" The monstrous creature might have easily crushed her beneath its feet, but terror of the spider kept Pen occupied.

The doppelganger began to shift shapes quickly, trying to find a protective form with which he might escape Eightball. He became several different fantastic creatures in a matter of seconds; including a Mothman, a Mongolian death-worm, an orangutaur, and a Sasquatch. None of these helped him escape the spider until he turned into a simple desert tortoise and hid himself in his shell. The spider rested on its back.

"Stay there, Eightball!" Eerey ordered. "I need to see what happened to Edict!"

"Go ahead," Mr. Cryptic said as she ran by. "I will take care of Pen."

Eerey rushed over the bridge, and breathed a sigh of relief to see Loofah pulling Edict away from the river of lava. "He almost fell in," the orangutaur informed her as she rushed over.

Eerey slowed her pace as she saw Edict. She didn't want to show too much concern. "I see you made it out just fine."

"I'm okay, just a bit bruised."

She smiled wryly. "Thanks for trying to save me. It was brave; for a boy."

"Yeah?" He smiled as he stood to his feet. "I couldn't do anything less for my favorite cousin, but what about you? You tried beating a gigantic dinosaur with your fists to save me! It wouldn't have helped, you know," He smiled. "But the effort is greatly appreciated!"

Eerey laughed. "I wasn't afraid of that old dinosaur!"

Edict grabbed Eerey and gave her a big hug. "I'm happy you're my cousin, Eerey!"

When Edict released her, Loofah said, "We've still got to flip the switches, and we still need one more to do it!"

The three of them heard a slight buzz coming from behind. "I'm here," they heard Guy's voice say. "I finally made it!"

"Whew!" Eerey expressed. "I'm glad you're here, Guy. I didn't want one more thing to deal with!" Despite her statement, they would have one more thing to deal with after they pulled the switches, but a time for everything and everything in its time.

"Well, let's not stand around here!" Edict said. "Let's get those switches pulled!"

They crossed the bridge and found Mr. Cryptic carrying Eightball on his shoulder. After regrouping, Mr. Cryptic showed them the room with the switches. They pulled on the switches, and the sluice closed. They averted the danger to the island, just as it had started, with a flick of a switch. The ground stopped shaking, and the volcano stopped pouring smoke.

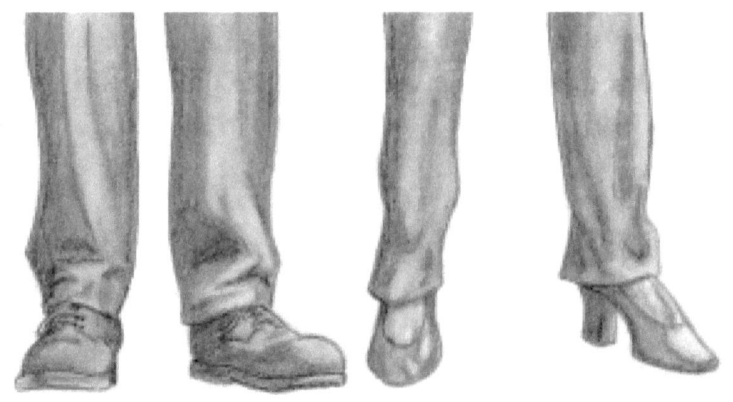

Eerey's Parents

CHAPTER XIX
THE DOPPLEGANGER'S DOWNFALL

Eerey turned to Mr. Cryptic. "What happened to Pen?"

"Nothing," Mr. Cryptic replied.

Edict's eyes grew wide. "You let him get away? After all that?"

Mr. Cryptic laughed. "I said nothing happened to him, and nothing did happen to him." Mr. Cryptic reached into his pocket and pulled out a small glass vial. A red stopper kept the top closed as a round, white light floated inside. The light moved inside the vial like an angry bee. "He's right here, as healthy as the day he was born."

"That's just a light!" Loofah huffed. "That's not Pen!"

Mr. Cryptic turned to Eerey. "Do you agree?"

Eerey slowly shook her head. "I think that's a will-o-wisp."

"A will-o-wisp!" Loofah laughed. "They're just a myth about tiny creatures of pure energy! They don't even exist!"

"I would have said the same thing about orangutaurs not so long ago," Edict reminded. He turned to Mr. Cryptic. "But why is he a will-o-wisp now?"

"As I predicted, Pen would change into something he thought Eightball could never get at." Mr. Cryptic held the vial above his head and peered into it. "A will-o-wisp was the obvious choice. He had gotten the DNA from one in the zoo's hospital."

"Couldn't he just turn into something larger and break out of the vial?" Guy asked.

Mr. Cryptic shook his head. "If he turned into something soft like a sponge, he'd just fill the vial and not be able to break out. He could change into a larger animal, but a doppelganger's bones are soft when they are forming into something else." He shook his head. "His organs would be vital, and he'd be crushed to death before he broke the glass or seal."

"So he's trapped in there," Loofah decided. Mr. Cryptic nodded in agreement.

"What will you do with him now?" Edict asked.

Mr. Cryptic shrugged. "I do not need to do anything with him right now," he replied. "I'll have to wait for a week or two to let the DNA he's ingested work its way out of him again. Then, I will have to banish him from the island."

"He will just come back," Eerey reminded.

"Not if I mesmerize him into forgetting the zoo's location," Mr. Cryptic replied. "He will be harmless then."

Guy sighed with relief. "Then I guess it's all over with."

"Not quite," Mr. Cryptic said. "We still have to get you all back home."

"I can't go back home," Loofah protested. "I want to stay here!"

"Yes," Guy agreed. "I want to stay too."

"You both are welcome to stay, of course," Mr. Cryptic said. "That just leaves the Tocsins. How are we to get you home?"

Right then it was time for the one more thing Eerey had hoped wouldn't happen.

"Shhhh!" Loofah demanded. He turned his head and listened for a moment. "What's that sound?"

Everyone listened intently. Finally, Edict said, "It sounds like an airplane with engine trouble!"

"Oh no," Mr. Cryptic said. "Someone must have drifted into the magnetic field!"

They all rushed outside to see a large plane painted olive drab struggling to stay aloft in the darkened sky filled with dense, acrid, volcanic smoke. It regularly disappeared between the clouds of ash only to appear again in another spot.

"That's a B-17 Bomber!" Edict shouted. "They used those in World War two!"

Mr. Cryptic shook his head at the scene. "You are correct, Edict. Unfortunately, that one will crash unless we help it."

"How can we help?" Eerey asked.

Mr. Cryptic began running. "Follow me! We need Atlanta, and she is close!"

They all followed Mr. Cryptic. After about five minutes of running, listening to the sound of the struggling engines the entire time, and hoping the sound didn't stop, Eerey saw the landing area where the giant bird had set her crate down. "There it is!"

Mr. Cryptic nodded. "And there's Atlanta."

"I know Atlanta's strong," Eerey began, "but can she lift an entire bomber by herself?"

"You are right, Eerey," Mr. Cryptic replied. "She can't do it alone. There are some weather balloons in that shed there. We use them for experimentation. Loofah and Edict, can you retrieve them and as many containers of air as you can carry?"

Edict offered Mr. Cryptic a clumsy salute. "Yes sir!" he said. He and Loofah rushed to the shed and began gathering the empty balloons as Eerey and Mr. Cryptic went to Atlanta. Mr. Cryptic spoke to the gigantic bird for a moment. It stooped to allow him and Eerey to climb onto its back.

Loofah and Edict soon returned with their arms full of deflated balloons and air canisters. Loofah had some difficulty climbing onto the bird's back, but soon all were aboard. Atlanta spread her enormous wings and flapped them. A violent wind came from the flapping wings.

"Hang on!" Mr. Cryptic shouted as the bird took to the air. The wind tore at them as the bird sped up to catch the plane, making their eyes water.

Atlanta flew directly to the flailing aircraft. Apparently, a bird the size of the plane made the pilot uncomfortable. He attempted some maneuvers to avoid Atlanta, but his engines did not cooperate. In fact, they sputtered for a moment and fell silent. The bomber's engines finally succumbed to the magnetic properties of the island. The fate of the craft was now up to the gigantic bird and the odd assortment of passengers it carried.

Atlanta straddled the plane's fuselage and wrapped her enormous claws around each of its wings. She glided along with the plane, gently guiding its path. The behemothian bird held her wings out to create wind resistance and slow the plane.

When the plane slowed considerably, Mr. Cryptic said, "Now we use the balloons. Loofah, you must stay here, as you could lose your footing and fall off."

Loofah dug his fingers into the soft feathers of Atlanta's back and gritted his teeth. "What? Do you hear me arguing?"

Mr. Cryptic continued, "I will go first to open the hatch on the top of the plane. Everyone else, carry as many balloons and canisters as possible. We need to get into the airplane. We'll fill the balloons inside. That should give Atlanta enough lift to help the plane glide to the ground. She can't hold it up for long as it is."

"We're ready, Mister Cryptic!" Guy shouted. The Tocsin cousins nodded. Edict handed Mr. Cryptic the end of Loofah's rope. "Tie it off inside!"

"Good thinking!" Mr. Cryptic replied as he took the end of the rope. He took a deep breath. "Well, here goes!" He carefully climbed down Atlanta's back and onto the surface of the plane.

Mr. Cryptic found the hatch and pulled at the handle. The wind pushed the hatch open violently, almost hitting the odd curator in the head. Mr. Cryptic climbed inside and quickly found a piece of metal and attached the rope. He gently pulled it a few times to let the others know that he'd secured it inside.

"Well!" Edict shouted. "That's our signal! Are you ready Eerey!"

"No!" Eerey shouted as she held her eyes shut tightly. "I'm not ready!"

"None of us are ready!" Guy shouted. "It can't be helped! We came here to help someone else!"

Eerey nodded. "I know!"

"Here!" Edict said. "Tie this rope around yourself!"

Eerey tied the rope around her waist and attached four canisters to it.

"No Eerey!" Edict protested. "You can't carry all those!"

"I can!" Eerey replied. "I'm your cousin. Just trust me!"

Edict looked at his cousin in astonishment. Finally, he smiled at her. His expression beamed with pride. "I trust you! I'll hold onto the rope and keep it steady!"

Eerey nodded. She closed her eyes and breathed deeply before beginning the journey.

Loofah commented, "That's the same rope you said wouldn't do any good!"

"It's no time to gloat!" Edict shouted to the orangutaur. "Save that for later!"

Eerey carefully began crawling down Atlanta's back. She crawled across the fuselage and slid into the hatch. Edict watched as Guy followed her, carrying a pair of air canisters under one arm. He couldn't see Guy, but he could see the canisters.

When the invisible boy disappeared through the hatch, it was Edict's turn. He took a deep breath along with a handful of balloons and followed the others. He carefully climbed toward the hatch. Suddenly, a gust of wind rose and pushed Atlanta and the airplane sideways. Edict screamed as he fell off the roof of the bomber.

Eerey didn't hear Edict's scream as the plane went sideways. The tilting sent her, Guy, and Mr. Cryptic crashing into the wall of the aircraft. Luckily, there weren't any loose items in the craft to fall on them and injure them.

Eerey saw that something pulled the rope taut, and figured Edict was the weight on its end. "Edict!" She turned to Mr. Cryptic and Guy. "Start filling the balloons! I'll check on Edict!"

The two nodded and began immediately filling the balloons. Eerey climbed the now-sideways ladder to the top hatch. She stuck her head out the opening and saw Edict holding onto the rope. "Hang on Edict!" she shouted.

Edict looked down to watch the ground far below move quickly by. "I don't have much else to do right now! Hurry!"

"He's on the end of the rope!" Eerey said. "Can we pull him in?"

Mr. Cryptic shook his head. "I would not trust that rope! It would break before he got in!"

Eerey looked around the interior of the plane. Finally, she found what she was looking for. She took her backpack off and grabbed the parachute. Then she climbed back to the top hatch, holding her backpack in her hand. "When you run out of balloons, pull the rope in!"

"Eerey!" Mr. Cryptic shouted. It was too late. Eerey crawled out the hatch and down the rope.

Edict saw her climbing toward him. "What are you doing! The rope might not be able to hold us both!"

"It will only have to for a minute!" she yelled. She reached the end of the rope. "Hold onto me tight!" Edict obeyed his cousin's orders with implicit trust, wrapping his arms and legs around his cousin as she held onto the rope with one hand. With her free hand, she took a pair of scissors out of her backpack.

"What are you doing!" Edict asked.

"I'm cutting the cord!" she yelled. She used the scissors to cut them loose from the rope. They both yelled as they started a free-fall toward the ground. Eerey realized she didn't really know how to work the parachute. "Am I supposed to pull something!" she asked.

"You mean you don't know!" Edict replied. "Never mind! Just look for a handle or something to pull!"

"What if I pull the wrong one!"

"What if you don't pull the right one!"

Eerey shrugged and began feeling around the parachute. Finally, she found something that felt like a large kite-handle. She pulled it.

For a moment, nothing happened. They continued to fall unchecked. Eerey looked at Edict, and Edict looked at his cousin. Then, a whooshing sound filled the air as the parachute opened.

They both laughed loudly as the parachute caught the air and yanked them upward. In her elation, Eerey forgot to look for a way to steer the parachute. It did not matter. After an unguided ride, they splashed into the lake where Eerey first saw Storsjöodjuret, or the lake monster called Judge. Eerey and Edict had a difficult but successful time disentangling themselves from the parachute.

As Eerey swam ashore with Edict after the exhilarating ride, she felt slightly disappointed she didn't see the lake monster. At the end of their swim they pulled onto the shore and sat down. They both watched the plane and the giant bird circling high above. The plane seemed much lighter, and Atlanta handled it with little difficulty. The giant bird and the aircraft were getting closer, and apparently coming in for a landing.

"Let's go see if everyone's okay," Edict suggested. They started walking toward the landing area where Atlanta had taken Eerey just the other night. It seemed that Atlanta meant to set the plane down there.

"You know Edict," Eerey said, "I couldn't have asked for a better cousin."

"Ditto that for me."

They watched Atlanta set the plane down gently as they walked toward the giant bird. The door on the side opened, and several weather balloons spilled out, rising into the air.

Eerey watched Guy come out first, followed by Mr. Cryptic.

"Guy!" Eerey shouted. "Mister Cryptic! You're safe!"

"We survived some scary moments," Mr. Cryptic replied. "We were more concerned about you two. I take it you parachuted down!"

"I don't think I could do that!" Guy said.

Eerey blushed. "We all did something dangerous today."

Atlanta landed nearby and allowed Loofah to climb off her back and end his harrowing experience. "If I'd been meant to fly," he said as he touched the ground, "I'd have wings already!"

"Loofah!" Edict shouted. "I'm glad to see you made it so you could gloat some more!"

"By the way," Guy said, "where is the plane's pilot?"

"I'm the pilot," a voice said. A man dressed in a dark green business suit pushed away more weather balloons and stepped out. A woman stepped out from behind him dressed in jeans and a t-shirt.

Eerey and Edict's eyes both widened. Eerey turned to her

friends and said, "It's my," she checked herself, "it's <u>our</u> parents." Her parents rushed to Eerey and Edict and hugged them both.

When her parents finally freed her from their clutches, Eerey retrieved her mother's sunglasses and put them on. "I knew you would do it, but how did you find us?"

"The post office tracked the crate you sent," Mr. Tocsin said. "They told us how they deliver air-mail to this address, and that there was no other way to communicate with the island, so I borrowed this plane from a friend to find you."

"What crate?" Edict asked.

"Forget it," Eerey said. "What matters is you found us!"

Vera Tocsin smiled. "Have we ever missed your birthday? We brought a cake and presents with us!"

"You didn't tell me it was your birthday," Loofah protested. "I didn't get you anything."

"We were kind of busy," Edict replied. "Besides, the rope was an excellent birthday present."

Mrs. Tocsin looked at Edict and Eerey. "Your clothes are ruined!" she exclaimed. The journey had turned Eerey's white dress into a dingy-gray dress. Straw covered Edict's wet, slightly-singed and torn suit. Both Eerey and Edict appeared quite disheveled, but very pleased with the turn of events.

"Don't be rude you two," Victor Tocsin said. "Introduce us to your friends!"

In the excitement, Eerey nearly forgot about the others. "Oh, this is our good friend Guy."

"Where?" Eerey's mother asked.

"He's right here," Edict replied, "but he's invisible."

Guy took Mrs. Tocsin's hand and shook it. "Pleased to meet you."

She was surprised at first, but she smiled at Guy. "I'm pleased to meet you as well." Mr. Tocsin found Guy's unseen hand and gave it a hearty shake.

"And this is Loofah," Edict said.

Loofah smiled broadly. "I'm an orangutaur," he informed them.

"Pleased to meet you, Loofah," Mrs. Tocsin said.

Mr. Tocsin took Loofah's hand and shook it. "I've been an astronomer all my life, but I've never seen an orangutaur before," he said.

"And I've never met an astronaut before," Loofah said with a smile.

"And this is Mister Cryptic," Eerey introduced the zoo's curator. "He helped us save you."

"Is that so?" Mr. Tocsin said as he shook Mr. Cryptic's hand. "I've got a bone to pick with you, endangering my daughter and nephew like that!"

Mr. Cryptic only smiled. "I assure you, if they had not stepped up themselves, I would not have been able to protect them from all the dangers they faced. You should be proud of Eerey and Edict."

"Oh, we are!" Mrs. Tocsin replied. "And thank you for watching out for them!"

"We watched out for each other," Eerey inserted.

Mr. Tocsin laughed. "Yes, and I am proud of you both! I think it's time to celebrate with cake and presents!"

"I am hungry," Edict admitted, "but I don't think presents will be as great as what we have standing right here."

Either no one present knew what the future would bring, or no one present would say what the future would bring, but right then, right there, they had friends and family with them. That was worth all the gold in the world. Despite this, Mr. Tocsin still retrieved the presents and cake and everyone enjoyed the party. Of all the moments in the Cryptoid Zoo, they would all remember this one for a long time to come.

end ?

About the Author

A friend to the Tocsin family, Kevin Noel Olson lives in Butte, Montana with his wife and other creatures. He researches Cryptoid animals he cannot find and writes short stories and long stories. His recent efforts include a Secret Agent X anthology and an interview with the famous film actor Robby the Robot. General consensus among his friends says that Kevin wouldn't hurt a fly, and that might well be true. Unless of course that fly is the size of a sedan and attacking him as food. In that case he would be forced to defend himself or others from bodily harm.

When the Tocsins decided to chronicle the adventures of their children Eerey and Edict, they approach Kevin with the project. This book now in your hands is the result of the pain-staking details drawn from Eerey's in-depth journals and eye-witness reports from creatures with multiple eyes. The only exception is the case of the Cyclops and his testimony. That is a singular viewpoint indeed.

www.ingramcontent.com/pod-product-compliance
Lightning Source LLC
Chambersburg PA
CBHW030508260626
47157CB00005B/1703